Tremble

....

Rose Akins

Contents

Chapter 1

"B lock him."

"Kill him."

"Punch him," yelled the barbaric and savage voices around me as I panted, and endeavored to block my opponent, who hurled solid blows at me. I rested my palm on my ear and rotated my body to the left side so that his strike would land on my bicep, and so it did. The punch did not sting much nor did the attack restrain me from planning my counter-strike.

The green Military t-shirt that barely hang like a pendant from my neck was torn and almost drenched in my crimson blood. Perspiration ran in rivulets down my head and sparkled under the hot sunlight. The dirt that engulfed both of us in a thick cloak made it hard to see or breathe.

"Kill him Blade, kill the moron," roared my best buddy Troy's voice from the throng that had gathered around us. They cheered and inspirited like ravenous beasts, barbarians that starved for a brawl.

I am sure you are well aware, of how it is when two men have a fistfight it's either 'Do or Die" The litter of hungry cubs congregated, and encouraged us. They gambled on who would be victorious. I or the moron who picked this fight, Maximus?

"You. shouldn't. have. done. that," I barked and pounded Maximus in the gut three times. With every blow, a whoosh of air escaped his lips, which contented me.

"What the hell!" he spat blood then licked the corner of his ripped, swollen lip. " Why shouldn't I? Huh? When I know your sister is sexy as hell, of course, I'll approach her," Maximus snarled, then clenched his stomach with a scarlet face, and huffed cheeks.

An animal-like growl sounded from my chest. I lifted my thigh and then slammed my patella, with fierce force in his face. Caught off guard he yelped, staggered then fell back to the ground. Without wasting any second, I lowered my body and pressed my combat shoe on his right shoulder. Then crushed my shoe harder in order to hinder him from standing up. I bent down so that our faces were mere inches apart.

"You know, you freaking know I will slaughter you if you lay your corrupted eyes on Maya ever again," my voice quivered with wrath, and my eyes blazed in fury. Maximus attempted to stand up but I was quicker. Promptly, in a swift movement, I rested my leg on his chest so that I was on top of the rascal and landed strikes on his face one after the other, from all angles.

I grinned like a damned Cheshire cat when I witnessed him cough and spit blood again.

Hell, I was content!

"What the hell Blade! If you be an imbecile like this no man will ever want her or marry her, " Maximus growled, wrapped his bloody and wounded fingers around the fabric of my shirt, and shook me.

"Screw you. I am telling you, next time Maya visits and I see you near her, it will be your head," I bellowed, then resumed my punching.

There was a distant yell and call for something unfathomable and the cheers around us died down at once like the sky after a tempestuous storm. However, I didn't pay heed to it. Maximus swung his fist and threw some punches at me from any aperture he got and hell it throb. An icy feeling surged in my nose and it stung but my wrath was far more than that to feel the real blow. Although I did know this shit was going to ache immensely after a while.

We both tackled ourselves to the ground and rolled around a few times. Grasped each other's shirts, with scarlet faces and rapid breathing. Coated in blood, sweat, and dirt, not a good combination, if you ask me. Too engrossed in our own fight we didn't perceive that the Colonel had arrived, we didn't realize he glared down at us, we didn't discern he had come to announce our new expedition.

And I was doomed!

Instantly both me and Maximus were snatched by our backs and ripped off from each other, mercilessly. I glared at that snake, who wiped the blood from his lip with the back of his hand and glowered back at me. Ready to launch for round two, and hell yeah! I was ready to bang the scoundrel.

"What the hell is going on here?" hollered Sergeant major, Bill Rhodes, who stood beside Colonel with their hands on their back, both with grim faces, clearly disenchanted. I didn't reply, merely struggled to appease my untamed breathing which seemed too stubborn to listen. Bloody rebellion.

I swiftly glanced around and noticed our little cheerleaders stood straight with their heads held high and saluted for Colonel and

Sergeant major. My eyes fell upon Troy who smirked which said. 'Dude you are in deep shit.' I thrust the impulse to roll my eyes because at that very moment Colonel had chosen to look straight at me.

"Blade, son of 'Marshal' Devin west," he exhaled, then shook his head in despondency; "It's really disappointing to see you in this state, Solider." I didn't sigh but felt a pang of anxiety.

Colonel, James Black, a well-known gentleman not just in the army but among civilians as well and a good friend of my father's, 'Marshal' Devin West. That's why I have to restate again. I am doomed.

"Get clean, you both have some serious elucidating to do. Meet us in five minutes, a second behindhand and you can kiss this new operation goodbye, ladies," ordered sergeant major, in a brittle voice. I flinched ever so slightly at his last word. Maximus and I saluted for them but they barely spared us a glance and marched away.

Once out of earshot my head snapped towards Maximus and I narrowed my eyes at him. His jaw clenched, sure the moron was a principled man but no one dared to pester my baby sister. He, on the other hand, actually dared to lay his impure hands on her in a not-so-decent manner. Something fractured within me and I lost my temper as soon as Maya had departed.

As soldiers, I don't think it's sagacious for me to fight with my team comrade, but sometimes they just shove in a thick stick up your backside and trust me you have to yelp.

I took a menacing step toward him, but a rough, large hand on my bare chest pushed me back. "Whoa calm down Blade. You heard the Captain, he demanded your presence there as soon as possible. Commence the show here again and you are toasted," Troy reminded me, shoving me backward again with a look in his eyes, a look he always provided to mollify my inner hellhound.

I pointed my finger at Maximus, "This time you're off the hook, next time I won't guarantee it. Go near Maya I'll make sure to chop your balls off." With that, I strode towards the washroom to rinse off blood from my face in order to meet up with Colonel and Sergeant Major.

Chapter 2

Once mud, blood, and sweat were cleansed from my hands and face. I forced my body to march towards Sergeant major's office instantly.

One minute and three seconds left.

A lethal glower made its way on my face when I spotted Maximus saunter from the other side of the hallway. Like he clasped the freaking globe on his palm. Just the sight of him caused the mishap which occurred an hour ago, displayed before my eyes.

Maya had come to visit before she departed the country for a week or so. I am well aware of how the men here ogle at her when she visits me. Her grace and splendor are my grave enemies. She inherited her beauty from our dearest mother. May God rest her soul in peace!

Shielding her from the indecent and lascivious beasts was arduous. I know what goes around in their vulgar minds because I am a damn man as well. Those immoral considerations for my sister scorch my skin.

And today, Maximus had an opportunity when I was a bit occupied in other matters to meet her. I had stepped into the scene and glared at the blockhead, but instead of being agitated, the imbecile had the audacity to actually smirk at me. God knew how I had restrained myself from thrashing him right in front of Maya. She would have abhorred that. Maya is hostile to aggression profoundly and I didn't want to distress her when she was about to leave for a week.

When she departed I did what I had to do and you know the rest.

I inhaled, tamed my impulse to punch him there, and then, instead decided against it. He has had enough for one day. I looked away from him and then gently tapped on the door. After three seconds we both proceeded inside and stopped a foot or two away from the table behind which 'Colonel' sat. His thick fingers entwined and his chin rested on them. He looked at us like an enraged bull, ready to thrust his horns in our backsides any second.

I stomped my foot and saluted for them and Maximus mirrored my moves. We stood in attention with our heels together, legs and arms straight but not locked, our fingers curled so that the thumbs were pointed straight down, shoulders square, head and eyes straight forward, just the way we had been trained. I kept my eyes fixed on the portrait behind Colonel, my body taut and attentiveness on them.

"What is the cause behind your actions today, Soldiers?" demanded Colonel James in a stern voice.

None of us vocalized a word for a few good seconds. I didn't know how to apprise him that this prick beside me got too close to my sister against her will. Even though he knows Maya loathes him as much as I do. That was the main reason I flipped.

Eventually, I decided to respond, "Nothing important, sir," I peered at the portrait behind him.

"What the hell is that supposed to mean?"Colonel barked. It means whatever the hell you want it to mean, sir. I wanted to utter those words but didn't and knew I would welcome him to my death party if I summoned enough courage to say them.

"I want an answer as to why you boys were acting like recalcitrant cowboys?" I remained hushed, eyes averted from his sweltering gaze, which pierced a hole in my head.

Maximus flinched. If it weren't for him we wouldn't have been here, in bottomless shit! Colonel James exhaled. From the corner of my eyes, I saw him glance towards Sergeant major then back at us, at me to be more specific.

And here it comes.

"I was informed Maya was here," when those words left his mouth I met his gaze at last. Once again he exhaled. To my incredulity, he understood me too well and my possessiveness over Maya. Being a family friend he made sure to fathom our temperaments. I really have no freaking idea how this man does it, but he was good!

Silence lapsed between us, in which I returned my gaze back on the frame and merely breathed and blinked.

Colonel James leaned back on his chair and rubbed his chin with thick fingers, "Unfortunately you two cowboys are matchless in this squad. I would very much like to see you sit at home and cook but the team needs you. That is why I am being tolerant enough to let this foolishness go, only this once," he paused. "Next time, any funny business from you soldiers and I'll make sure you stay at home," he growled.

"Yes sir," we both responded in unison. Grateful that we were off the hook and at the same time exuberant for the new expedition.

"Dismissed," incensed Bull, ordered.

With a farewell salute, we headed to the door but were halted when Sergeant major spoke; "Gentlemen, I would like both of you to do five laps around the camp," he stared at us. "And yes with your luggage," and added, with a villainous, nasty smirk.

I literally sighed but ended up with a "Roger that," and evacuated the room. Once out I twirled to the other side not really in a mood to talk to this dip-shit.

"Yo Blade," Maximus called.

With an exasperated sigh I turned to give him a deadly glare which made him smirk; "Have a nice run." He snickered.

I clenched my fist desiring to give his other eye another purple glory instead, I rotated and strode away. The numbskull knows I respect this occupation more than him and prick always testes my forbearance.

I must have forgotten to divulge that this camp was humongous. Five laps around it are a painful and strenuous task and I should add with my darn luggage. We live, practice, and train in barracks to keep our bodies in shape and it takes nearly all our time.

I slung my luggage over my shoulders with a scowl. Then launched into the laps, and so time dragged. My body was already exhausted from all the exertion, now this took the best of me. Fatigue rolled on my form in a chunky blanket by the time I was done. At three in the afternoon I finished the laps, sweating like a pig I reported back to Lieutenant.

I ambled into my room to get some rest. Something inside of me frowned and I slammed the door shut. Troy looked up from the book or whatever he was reading and hovered an eyebrow at me.

"I don't want your shit now," I growled, took off my shirt, and tossed it at him. He grimaced and flung it on the floor.

"Something crawled up your bum and bit it," he smirked. "Calm down man, being furious won't solve this, and yeah, daddy Colonel asked to inform you once you are back, to get ready they have to demonstrate the new mission," he apprised, resting his hands behind his head and peered at me.

"Give me five." was all I uttered before I went into the bathroom for a shower. When I was finished with the shower I took a glance in the mirror to see my reflection, not bad. Tall almost 6'3, my blonde hair was short very short just like all other soldiers. Azure eye color always allured the girls so I was fortunate to have them, and with all the training they make us do my body was in splendid shape.

By the time we crossed the threshold of the conference room, half of our squad was already present. Lights were dim with a projector screen on. Troy took a seat next to me and looked at daddy Colonel, who stood in front of us, as big bad wolf.

I placed my hand on the armchair, then pinned my full concentration on Colonel James. Twenty soldiers in this squad sat in the conference room along with twenty from the other team. They stared at Colonel and Lieutenant in determination and wholeheartedly.

Colonel James addressed us; "Well Soldiers, as you all know we are gathered here to apprise you about our new mission" tension rose up like a tick cloud and bodies went rigid. "This city called Empana is located on the West Coast. Unfortunately, the city has been taken over by terrorists and many killings have been reported to us," he turned his body to the side and pointed to the slide show which displayed images of destruction, in each slide there was blood and massacre. Buildings, schools, and hospitals were demolished. Bodies lay lifeless on streets drenched in crimson blood.

"Lieutenant Hayden's team along with other squads and mine will make an ambush," he looked at us. "In order to save as many people and lives as we can. These are orders from above," he explicated.

I knew very well that by 'above' he meant the 'The government' and my very own father, Marshal of our army. He is the only reason why I am here. My entire life I worked immensely hard to keep up with his glorified image.

"This mission will take some time we cannot predict how long, a month, two, or probably a year," my brows knit at this piece of information "No one has any idea how to differentiate between the civilians and the terrorists," he pursed his lips. "Our teams have to patrol day and night in order to find them and engage if need be," Colonel finished, leaned back on the table behind him, and peered at us with his hands crossed over his wide chest.

"Any questions?" Lieutenant demanded, stealing our attention from him.

"What are the rules of engagement?" inquired Troy.

"There are no rules," Lieutenant replied.

"Anything else?" repeated Colonel.

"No sir, " came deep, and low voices in unison.

"Dismissed, take the day off, "I raised my brow. "Tomorrow at dawn I want you all present here," Colonel commanded with a nod then headed to the door.

We lived in this Barrack and trained here non-stop. A day off gave us an opportunity to break out from the disciplined world to meet our families and go anywhere we fancied.

Troy and I wandered out of the camp with my knapsack in hand. "Where are you going now?" he questioned, tossed his car keys in the air then caught them.

"I'm not going to meet the angel of death (my father) not after he already knows what I did today," I replied, threw my knapsack on the backseat then slammed the door shut.

"Man, have some respect he is your old man," Troy chuckled.

I raised my eyebrows, "No, more like a grenade of intimidation," then laughed.

"So, where to?" he investigated once again as we sat in his car and drove away. I clench and unclenched my fist because it stung a little from the early fistfight.

"Someplace where I can calm myself. Maya would have done that but she ain't here," whenever I lose my temper her soothing words calmed my inner fiend, just like our mother used to do.

"What about the club?" Troy suggested.

"Don't know man, I'm pretty exhausted to go there and handle ladies," I mumbled, then rubbed a hand over my face.

"C'mon, it won't be that bad, and not every day we have a day off," he argued and spared me a glance.

"Fine man, whatever you say," I told him and the rest of the ride to his home was silent. I knew both of us were thinking about this new mission. Hell, it sounded hazardous but then again it was what we do. That is why we are called, daredevils.

Chapter 3

After only five hours of slumber, I woke up and cursed under my breath at the intense tingle in my left eye. Call me an early bird but I had to. I rubbed my eyes and got out of the bed, it was still three in the morning. The only source of light was from the bedside lamp that protected me from the wall I was about to collide into. My feet dragged behind me as I walked into Troy's room, the idiot was fast asleep, and snored like there was no tomorrow. His body splayed around the bed as if he had fallen from the sky. I shook my head disapprovingly and strolled up to him.

"Yo Troy, wake up man," I shook his arm.

Nothing.

A vexed sigh escaped my lips. Guess I have to try something different. An unholy smirk made its way on my face when I smacked the back of his head with force. With a 'What the f--k' he sat bolt straight on his bed and I guffawed at his expressions, which were extremely wacky.

"Man you are such a wimp. It's not like I flung a freaking grenade at you," I taunted in between laughs.

Troy glared at me like he couldn't believe it, "Piss off," he turned away from me.

"You wish," I snickered then rotated to switch on the light.

"Just for the record I sleep like an owl," he growled.

"Owls don't sleep at night you butt-head," I chuckled. "Now get your bum up, we have to go," I called over my shoulder at him and went to take a shower.

Time elapsed and twenty minutes later I was in my combat suit. All my stuff was sprawled on the bed and I eyed them. After a few seconds ticked by I grabbed my combat boots and wore them quickly then rose to my feet. I wore my cap and slung the bag over my shoulder.

Troy wore his military uniform as well. He lifted his head at my approach. "Ready?" I asked, and rolled my shoulders to ease off anxiety.

"Yeah," once out of the house, he took his time to lock the door behind him while I sat on the passenger's seat, waiting. Was he actually saying 'Goodbye' to his house? Troy drove fast once we hit the highway on a foggy night. Dawn was yet to break but for us, it still would be dark and gloomy, with death on our tail.

"Did Maya call?" my man interrogated when we neared the Air Base.

I gave a curt nod in reply. "I don't know if I will see her again," I murmured then cleared my throat.

Troy let out an exaggerated sigh, "C'mon man, don't even start this shit again. You always dart after death whenever we go on a new mission," he snapped.

I raised an eyebrow at him. "I am being serious here," and growled, then ran a hand on my scalp.

"Yeah right," he chuckled. I shook my head and decided to swap the topic.

"You talked to Jenny?" I veered the topic. She is the only family he has, his mother. Well, if you wanna call his creep of a brother who left them when he turned eighteen to enjoy what the world had to offer him. Then I guess he had a brother too.

"Yeah, man her tears almost drowned me." Troy laughed and stopped at a red signal.

Two hours later.

Troops sat in the military aircraft, which was filled with nothing but uncomfortable fierce apprehension. I glanced around and witnessed soldiers were set for it. If you ask me I knew every man was thinking about their loved ones. Will they ever be able to see them again?

I was among them as well. A picture of Maya was in my hands. I remember the time it was taken, when I had returned home from my very first mission. She had been exceedingly joyful and had invited all my friends for dinner. The picture I held was from the very same night. She was smiling here, her long brown hair that cascaded down on her shoulders, matched her brown eyes. She resembled our mother a lot. I suppose that's why both I and the old man were so attached to her.

Troy had fallen asleep almost an hour ago. I glared at him when his snoring hit my ears and disturbed my tranquillity. His seat was right next to mine, a little too close. Other soldiers either endeavored to get some rest or converse in hushed voices. I swept my eyes at the guys who accompanied me on this perilous mission. These men and women in the troops were now my family my brothers. They were my responsibility to shield and I was theirs.

I attempted to disregard the idiot beside me. I don't even know why I put up with his shit. Sure he knows me too well. I assume, even better than I know myself, secrets that I hide in a cave he somehow manages to locate!

After a while, I rubbed my hand over my face and then rested my head on the headrest. A few prolonged moments later my eyelids were heavy and sleep overtook my form and I welcomed it with open arms.

It wasn't going to do any good. Lamentably, my eyes would snap open every ten minutes, from anxiety, or dread. After about seven hours of constant torture and mental agony finally Lieutenant informed us that in five minutes the plane would land at the Air Base of Empana.

We were perturbed and frantic that we could die, but when we thought deeply about this situation. We were conceited to know that we would die for our families, friends, and our country. That we would die protecting someone, that we would fight till our last breath. The silence that had swelled in the aircraft had its own beauty as in that moment every soldier perceived why they were there. They were ready to face any obstacle in order to serve their country.

Soldiers rose to their feet, pride gleaming in their eyes. They wore their protections with many indescribable feelings that ran in their veins. They hung their rifles over their shoulders, all set. I looked at Troy, who stared at me with a smile on his lips.

"What?" I questioned, stood up to grab my Bullet-proof vest so I could fasten it around my chest. He copied my moves.

"Nothing," was all he uttered. I frowned at him but wasn't in a mood to inquire so I simply got back to work. It took me three minutes to wear my bullet-proof vest as everything had to be on place.

I thrust my fingers in the gloves, pulled at them then wore my pistol holster on my right leg. When that was done I carefully mounted my knife in its sheath on my left calf and took hold of the dump pouch which was full of magazines. I wrapped it around my waist, and let it dangle on my left side so it would be easy to grab a magazine when I was out of bullets.

My water canteen pouch and aid kit were ready and placed where they belonged. I sat on my chair again a little uncomfortable with the stuff I was wearing and wrapped the knee pad inserts on my knees and stood up, ready to go. At last, I glanced over my shoulder to see Troy was almost set.

Our plane at last landed and doors opened to allow fresh air along with yellow rays of the afternoon sunshine to seep into the plane. Troops got out of the plane in a line and soon were divided into four squads. Each squad was of twelve men along with their squad leaders. Zach, an extremely tall and bulky man, with black hair and a light goatee, stood in front of us. He, the leader of the squad, examined us.

"Soldiers get ready," yelled Lieutenant Hayden to all squad members over the loud chopping of 'The Black Hawks' which stood about fifty meters away. Soldiers marched up to them and slightly lowered their heads. I tightened my grip on my 'M16 assault Rifle" and followed them. With every step that I took my strength awakened even further.

Moments before we engaged in combat believe me it was not a nice feeling. You feel apprehensive, timorous, and distressed and at the same time, you feel blessed and divine that you were doing this for your people. You feel mighty, and your feelings escalate and fluctuate from one to another in a blink of an eye.

Every member went through different feelings, some burned with rage while others recalled the faces of their beloved ones. My ticker beat dangerously rapid and trashed against its cage but I kept a straight face. I had to keep a straight face. The days of dread will soon be over, but for now, right here, this moment my duty comes first even before my life. I shoved all my agitation into the depth of my heart and embraced courage. I embraced death.

Deserted land whizzed by us for a long time, but then we saw it, saw smoke that clouded the entire city. Bodies lay deceased and cold on the streets. People dashed away in order to hide for their lives. Guns blazed and huge blasts were heard.

The pilot to the right signaled that we have arrived and it was time to face the massacre. Thick, heavy ropes were thrown down from the chopper that hovered. It was time for us to descend.

With the help of fast-roping, Zach, our squad leader was the first to go down followed by Troy and three others. After a minute I followed them. They had already taken their positions, looking out for any sort of hazard as the others descended.

I drew my gun and stood behind Zach, ready to pull the trigger, ready to attack. Pure adrenaline, the rush of being challenged simmered in my blood. My pulse was fast and sweat drizzled down my forehead.

Once we were done with our positions and prepared to act. Black Hawk hovered high in the sky, indicating that it was time for us to move!

When Zach had signaled to move my squad proceeded forward gradually. I notice how immensely destroyed this place was. Buildings and shops were almost transformed into dust. The remaining of walls had holes in them, which clearly meant some heartless monsters none stop emptying their magazines here. There were demolished cars on the roads and dried blood all around us, the abhorrent smell almost suffocated me.

The squad kept walking past the ruined walls, with our weapons drawn. We endeavored to hear every sound, but none was heard other than the furious wind that swayed around us.

The afternoon sun scorched the ground and it felt like we have come to a place where there was no existence of human beings. Those demonic terrorists were the ones who caused this. If not much I will cherish annihilating those monsters who slaughter innocents.

Troy and I walked together. None of us had vocalized a word since we arrived here in this human-made hell hole.

"See this?" he jerked his chin to a burnt van.

"I don't understand those demons. Why would they do this? If they have some issues they could tackle them with the government why kill innocents?" I growled.

"That's what they do, man. That's what the monsters do," Troy replied, remorsefully.

Uncountable minutes had passed and we kept walking. Every time we turned a corner the squad would stand against a ruined wall to wait while Zach or some other member would lookout for any sort of peril that lurked in the shadows of the buildings. When everything was clear orders were given out to move again. At times like this, each man begins to feel that someone out there would aim at him ready to pull the trigger at any time. This is very nerve-wracking, to say the least!

We would hear guns blaze from far away but did not halt. Now and then the earth beneath our feet would tremble we still did not cease our movements. Residents ignored us with horrific looks on their faces. It tugged on a heart to see them in this desolated condition.

Our squad walked past a shop, which was burned to ashes, few soldiers stared at it with distress and revolt noticeable on their faces. It was then hell broke on us, we had little time to react, little time to see that a large number of people had us on their target.

That's when guns started to roar and bullets passed us!

Chapter 4

He stood there, barrel of his gun pointed at me. I glared back at the large man who just like me was coated in grime and blood. Dread glimmered in his blue eyes. A deep miserable cut was drawn on the side of his cheek, which started from his cheekbone and disappeared in his thick beard.

I caught a glimpse of my death in his eyes, which made me swallow the lump that kindled my throat. My finger rested on the trigger but valor wasn't tough enough to pull the damn thing and get it over with. He yelled then pulled the trigger of his rifle. I merely stood there, waiting for the pain to greet me and for darkness to engulf me.

But it did not.

My eyes shot open to see that my enemy was out of bullets!

An inner voice howled within, so forceful and distraught that it jerked me out of my trance. Its intensity yanked me back to the blazing of guns. I was petrified at the same time I was livid. My opponent instantly tugged out his pistol to fire at me and that's when it happened. That's when my quivering finger pulled the trigger. Seconds later his body fell benumb on the grass.

He was the first man I killed.

It has been three horrendous and burdensome weeks since we came here to this city 'Empana'. My team patrolled day and night, under the sweltering sun. We felt exhausted, mentally knackered after twenty-one days of constant wretchedness. We'd take any opportunity we got to rest under a merciful tree or just the generous sky.

It commenced the very first day we set foot here, the 'killing'. We were ambushed by the enemies after only five hours of our arrival. Zach, the team leader was swift and quick-witted enough to assemble his men behind a shop and act. It wasn't uncomplicated, the enemy was many compared to our team. But still, luck was with us. We had annihilated many of those who desired to slaughter innocents, and trust me it isn't pleasant, killing a human is not pleasant. We remember the face of every man we kill and sometimes those faces are the ground behind our night terrors.

Every night we would get rest for about three or two hours, during which two comrades of the squad would stay up, alert, and look out for peril. Those hours were grievous, every second was utter depression and distress. There were times when none of us vocalized words, we would just scrub our guns, reload them and ponder. Think about anything but death.

End of the third week

Day: Friday

Time: 14:30

"What do you see?" Zach's voice sounded in my ear through the listening device.

I lay on my abdomen on the roof of a house, that faced directly a room in the enormous house opposite this one. I peered through the eyepiece of my rifle. We were apprised that there were hostages held in that house for over three days now and we had to rescue them without raising any alarm. They hadn't provided us with information on the number of hostages and the captors.

Zach had commanded me to get on the roof and study the scene then report back to him as soon as possible. The rest of my squad stayed behind, encompassing the building where the enemy held a few guiltless captives, waiting to charge.

"Three hostages, two females and a boy," I rammed the button of my throat microphone, eyes on the room on the second floor. There was a light bulb that dangled limply from an electrical flex from the center of the ceiling. The room appeared to be a study room, where two women were tied together in a corner, while the boy was tied to a chair at gunpoint.

The one that pointed the gun at the boy's head spoke to another, who stood guard by the door. His head was covered beneath a hood. Then he leaned forward to the boy's left ear and uttered something.

"I see four of them, two by the door. One in the room and the last one near the window within range," I once again pressed the button of the microphone.

"Roger that."

A few seconds proceeded in which I surveyed the hostages. They had clothes tied around their mouths. One of them had her head bowed, clearly exhausted and petrified, the other woman appeared to be rather old.

I frowned as the women wept and glanced at the boy. "Blade, take down the one within range when we go in, wait for my orders," Zach spoke in a low voice.

"Roger that, Sir," I replied, directing my gun at the captor alongside the window. Something ignited within me when the tears of the woman flashed before my eyes just by the sight of the terrorist. I could only make out his eyes as the rest of the scoundrel's face was hidden behind a bandanna.

"Go, go, go, go, weapons hot, weapons hot!" hollered Zach through the radio. I cringed a bit from the voice in my ear but didn't pay much heed to it.

The door burst open and our men marched in. Their arrival caught everyone off guard. The people in the room twirled to face my team. Some anticipated being rescued while others expected the worse. I kept my eyes on the man who yelled when my team barged in like death. I desired to see his face, wanted to know who it was I eliminated. With that I pulled the trigger, the bullet shattered the window and pierced a hole in his head, a moment later his dead body fell to the ground.

Promptly I pushed myself off the floor, slung my rifle over my shoulder, and darted downstairs. The stairs I dashed from were destroyed and so I made sure to be extra cautious. There was no sound and no one in the house, it was deserted. I wasn't surprised.

I sprinted out of the house I was in, then leaped over the fence, crossed the street, and entered the AO (Area of operation) where the hostages were held. Once again I hopped over the fence and bolted into the house. Carlos and Bruce, members of the squad stood by the door as guards.

Taking two steps at a time, I mounted the stairs and then stood at the door of the study room. Everything was hushed as though life after a lethal hurricane. Mason, Doc of our squad had already untied the boy. Zach advanced to untie the others. I stepped over the dead bodies and proceeded into the room.

"I will not hurt you," Zach vocalized gently to them. His eyes were on the girl who looked like she was in her late teen-ages. I heard her whimper, terrified as she stared at Zach's rifle.

Shit!

I glanced to my right to see Troy, he had a deep frown on his face as he watched, "Hold this for me." I whispered, handing him my rifle.

Troy looked at me questioningly. I shook my head in a way that said 'Will explain later.' Painstakingly I walked up to where they were, then spared a quick glance at the captor I had just shot dead a few minutes ago. Then I stood next to Zach.

"Sir," I called for his attention breaking the tension. He looked at me with his eyes slightly narrowed. I hinted with my eyes towards Zach's rifle, he cursed under his breath and took a step back, in order to let me handle this plight.

I inhaled a deep breath, took off my helmet, and bent down so that I and the girl were at eye level. Her green eyes met mine. Something like a wave hit me. There was an ocean of dread and terror that swam in them, and the tears that played on her lashes tugged at my heart.

"There-" I was cut off when she hiccuped and more tears rushed down her eyes. It took all my might to not frown and to keep a straight face. She was scared of me. I wouldn't even dream of hurting them or her!

"Everything is okay, they are gone, no one here will harm any of you. I promise, please let us aid you," I begged without breaking eye contact. At first, she didn't seem to trust me, her green eyes displayed many things yet they were unheard. There was a grisly gash on her temple and blood had dried there, on the spot. Her brown hair was dirty and tangled, which curtained the side of her face. Blood dripped from the ghastly cut on her lip.

Gradually, almost dubious she nodded then dropped her gaze. I rose to my feet, seized hold of my knife then cut the ropes and loosened the cloth around their mouths. Mason instantly marched up to them. The women looked at him with wide eyes, that brimmed with disquiet. "Ma'am I am a doctor. Please let me aid your wounds," he pleaded, tenderly.

The woman gave a curt nod but the girl bit her lip and crawled back, clearly not trusting him. Mason begin with his task and I rotated around to look at Zach.

"Good job," he praised. I bobbed my head as thanks. The little boy ran up to the woman and engulfed her form in his small arms. I assumed he was his mother, while the girl stared down. Maybe she had her own story.

"Sir, you better have a look at this," Troy popped his head from the door. I hadn't perceived he had evacuated the room. Zach nodded and followed I walked behind him. Troy led us to the room on our right. The half-broken door was ajar. As we got closer it got harder to breathe, the place reeked like Hell.

"Shit," Zach hissed at the scene in front of him. I covered my nose with my hand and then gritted my teeth.

Four dead bodies lay lifeless on the bed, drenched in their own blood. The smell meant this has happened days ago. I walked further into the room behind Zach, wrath seethed in me. At that moment I really wanted to kill someone.

I closed my eyes at the sight before me. Among them was a young girl they had murdered. Those monsters had emptied an entire magazine into the girl's body! I rubbed my head with my left hand and stared at the bodies. They must be the owners of this house.

Zach hovered over the little girl's body, he bent down, enfolded the baby's body in a quilt, and rose, her tiny hand dangled, limp, soulless. After a moment of staring at her, Zach brought her closer to his chest, inhaled, and kissed her bloody hair. He then rotated slowly, his hand tightened around the quilt as he lay the tiny form next to the other dead bodies and I know he had tears in his eyes. I clenched my jaw and studied the room, my main aim was to not look at them anymore.

A loud shriek made us all twirl towards the source. The girl we just rescued ran in when her eyes witnessed the bodies. I took a step forward, ready to prevent her from getting any closer to the bodies.

It was then Troy appeared from behind her and cloaked his hands around her waist. She pushed on Troy's hands and screamed even louder, her eyes darted from one body to another. Screw it! They were her family; the dead bodies belonged to her beloved ones.

Tears streamed down from her puffy and red eyes, as she sobbed harder. Suddenly her body gave in, completely paralyzed and she begin to collapse. Troy held her shoulders in a firm, yet gentle grip and raised her up. Her head bowed and silent tears trickled down her green eyes. I licked my dried lips and again rubbed my temple.

"Get her the hell outta here," Zach barked, with a nod Troy gently dragged the worn-out, horrified, and lost girl who had almost faced death and had cheated it, out of the room.

"What now?" I quietly asked Zach, in an attempt to ignore the wailing girl.

"We all get the hell out of here. Keep them with us till the choppers are ready. Lieutenant Hayden has informed us to return back to the FOB (forward operating base) another team would be sent to patrol on our behalf, now move." he replied, didn't spare a glance at the bodies, and got out of there.

After two hours of traumatic walk. We, soldiers, kept the refugees in the midst of our circle so that they were shielded, while we looked out for lurking danger, and thankfully we hadn't crossed paths with any.

Eventually, my team reached the place where 'Black hawks' would escort us back to the Base. Zach, Carlos, and Bruce stayed with the refugees. Meanwhile Troy, Mason, and I settled in the other Helicopter.

I glanced up at Mason, our doc, who had a somber and woeful look on his face. I had never seen him like this. The man was the most exuberant and honest person I had ever encountered in my life. He was damn committed to his all-time girlfriend and now wife and mother of his baby girl. It isn't hard to guess that he was thinking about them right now.

When the bird hovered in the sky I couldn't help but to crave for the day this will be over.

"What's all that about?" I investigated as we strolled towards the tents. I don't know about others but I practically dragged my feet from exhaustion.

"A refugee camp for the residence. We have also been ordered to protect them," Zach answered, with a jerk of his head towards the innumerable camps next to the army base almost a mile or so away.

"The refugees that we've been saving?" Mason inquired, eyebrows raised.

"Yes," Zach replied impassively. I glanced at Troy who had a frown, eyes fixed on the camps and I comprehended why he wore such a face.

"You're shitting me right?" I hissed and hoisted my eyebrows.

He shook his head "No man, I am not. Other troops still haven't arrived, and I am sure they want protection. There are chances for us to patrol there," Troy explained.

"I'm exhausted," Mason complained.

So am I!

"Let's see what happens," I uttered, then glanced over the camp. Suddenly a face materialized before my eyes, a face that belonged to the girl with green eyes. I shook my head and followed the men.

Finally being back on the Base felt pleasant in its own way, but we were still vigilance all the time, always prepared for danger. We could not help but feel that way everywhere. It's what we do. It's who we are. After I took a shower, well I won't actually call it a shower but still. When dirt and blood were washed off the skin, it breathed fresh air again.

Once that was done. I went into the tent which had up to twenty bunk beds. Everyone was already asleep because our squad had arrived here after 1:00 o'clock. As for my buddy, Troy, he sat on his bed with his body tilted and drooled in his sleep. I wouldn't blame the guy he needed that, needed some rest on a soft pillow.

Someone walked into the tent that very moment and halted a foot or two away from my bed. I hopped to my feet only to come face-to-face with Zach.

Why is he here?

"You both get ready and come with me," was all he pronounced and departed from the tent. I glanced back at Troy over my shoulder.

He arched an eyebrow, vexed. Once we were in our combat clothes, rifles slung over shoulders we left the tent. Troy and I walked out of the tent and found Zach waiting for us in heavy rain.

We both stood there and got soaked as the furious wind blew raindrops, and the lighting struck; "Two men have been chosen from each squad to patrol the night at the refugee camp and you both have been picked from my team," Zach spoke the words loud and clear. His eyes on us and didn't even blink. I knew Troy was incensed I could sense it rolling out into invisible fumes. As for me I just desired to rest.

"Am I clear?" Zach repeated himself when none of us answered or gave a nod.

"Yes sir," here we both replied in unison.

There were six chosen men from each squad. They stood there waiting to move, none of them vocalized a word. I was more than certain they were not disposed about this because squads had just returned from their onerous missions and this was just what we did not need.

"Come on it's not that bad," Troy mimicked Maximus in a frustrated growl. Maximus had said those words to him a few minutes ago. Regrettably, he was with us too, like Colonel mentioned that moron was among the best of his men. I chuckled and proceeded behind our little new team towards the camp gates.

"Maximus is right, it's not that bad," I stated, more like endeavored to coax.

"You don't start now," Troy hissed and I smirked.

Heavy and severe raindrops fell on the roof of the tent which made it exceedingly strident. Trust me I did not give a shit about it. The night sky glistered whenever lightning struck. I rubbed my eyes with the back of my hand and attempted to get some freaking rest. It was time for me and Troy to get some sleep while others patrolled. I was certain it was near dusk and tomorrow at noon we had to depart again.

F--k my Luck!

The lids of my eyes got heavier with each second that passed. Whenever I decided to close them I just couldn't sleep. Even though every single vanquished bone in my body was in agony. It howled to get some rest. Troy had fallen asleep long ago on the chair in a very uncomfortable posture.

My eyes shut themselves after a while but opened once again, with a tremendous effort, at last, I rested them for the best and the world begin to hush very gently as the heavy raindrops had transformed into a lullaby. That's when there was an ear-piercing scream which rang in the air louder than a clap of thunder. I sat bolt straight on my chair and looked around.

Nothing. Maybe I was hallucinating? Or maybe it was just the wind playing dirty tricks? I grabbed a plastic bottle next to me and flung it at Troy. It hit him square in his head. The man jerked with his fists clenched to punch whoever the hell it was here to kill him.

"Did you hear that?" I questioned in a hushed voice.

"Hear what?" He opened his fists and peered at me.

"The scream,"

"I didn't hear anything. I was freaking sleeping," he growled. "My dearest Florence Nightingale turn off your freaking lamp and get some darn rest we have a long day ahead of us," Troy added, then threw his head back to rest. When his head was an inch away from the plastic chair there it was again.

A desperate and anguished yell!

Both of us stood up instantly, with deep frowns on our faces. Troy snatched his pistol and I darted out of the tent with him, hot on my heels. This yell sounded from somewhere close almost from behind our tent. I disregarded the wrathful clouds and the mud that kissed my shoes. Something inside my chest clawed at my heart and a grievous feeling blazed within me so I strode forward.

Without a warning or any precaution, I turned the corner to see two men, they circled something or someone. Then I took a few steps forward to see what was happening, and that's when I froze.

Chapter 5

- -

Both of us stood up in a blink of an eye with deep frowns on our faces. Troy snatched his pistol and I dashed out of the tent with him, hot on my heels. The yell sounded from somewhere close, almost from behind our tent. I disregarded the wrathful clouds and the mud that kissed my shoes. Something inside my chest clawed at my heart and a grievous feeling blazed within me so I strode forward.

Without any warning or precaution I turned the corner to see two men, they circled something or someone. I took a few steps forward to see what was happening, and that's when I froze.

There was a girl! Her clothes were soaked in rain and the hair that stuck on her face curtained it from sight. She struggled against someone's rough grip enfolded on her waist as crimson blood oozed from the wound on her right thigh, her blood fell drop by drop on the mud. The girl's shoulders quivered and I discerned that she wept. She was petrified.

What the hell is she doing here? And who the hell is she?

I glanced up to see Lee, the well-known man-whore. He grinned down at his prey, I knew he was drunk. He obviously attempted to get some pleasure from the girl who stood there terror-stricken. I growled at the sight and noticed from the corner of my eyes that Troy curled his hands in fists too. Fury radiated from his body. I had to do something and do it swiftly.

"Let her go, Lee," my voice threatened as I took a few steps forward.

Lee glared at me with a savage look in his eyes, "Ladies and gentlemen, the mighty Blade," he hissed and chortled like the pig that he was. His laugh made the girl sob harder. Her petrified voice and his maniac laughter fulminated wrath further in my blood. I still couldn't make out her face, her head was hung low. She probably prayed this was all a dream, a horrendous nightmare.

"Why is it? Why is it that whenever there is something going on you bloody appear?" Lee turned to me. "Don't you freaking dare meddle in my affairs, Blade. I won't let you, not today," he barked, then grabbed a chunk of the girl's hair and jerked it back with force so that her face was revealed to me and my eyes popped out of their sockets.

The ground underneath my feet cracked open and it's conflagration blazed within me, just by sight of her innocent face. It was her, the girl with the green eyes, we saved hours ago! Her glassy eyes fell upon me. The girl blinked few times to clear her vision, her eyes pleaded us to shield her from the fiend. Then, swiftly a look of recognition appeared in them when she recalled who I was.

The imbecile had no idea that this, very girl had lost her whole family in a blink of an eye. That she had witnessed their bodies that were pierced with incalculable bullets. That she was almost murdered by those vicious terrorists and yet his repulsive desire urged him to chose this sinless girl.

I trailed my eyes to look at Lee and took another step towards his death. A thunder decided to sound at that time and the girl screamed both from the huge rumble and Lee's face that neared hers. Now that I was a foot or two away from them, her silent whimpers reached my ears.

"I am giving you few seconds Lee. If you don't let the girl go, I won't be responsible for the outcome," the voice that I spoke in was foreign to me, like some sort of malicious in my heart had just stirred. Lee snickered in a pitched voice and then flashed a drunk smile like he didn't believe my threat was serious.

Seconds ticked and tension got thicker.

"Lee don't do this. You will regret it once you are sober," Chase a friend of this moron suggested. Lee shook his head in disagreement like a pathetic kid. At that moment I thrust the urge to put my gun on his head and flex my finger on the damn trigger.

"Chase is right Lee. You will regret this later on and beside I don't think you have a chance on getting away from us," Troy attempted to coax him without any harm and damage. If we leap in action we would be investigated for our actions and probably they will inculpate us guilty because Lee is drunk and has lost his senses long ago. So we had to talk the dullard out of this.

"Get the hell away from me, you sick rats," Lee hollered, pressed the girl closer to his body and took a small step back.

I braced myself to punch the day lights off from this pig that's when the girl gasped and her head rolled back. I darted over to them, my steps fast as lighting and punched Lee straight in the face. He staggered back and let go of the girl. Her body swayed in the air, promptly I snaked my arms protectively around her and stopped just when I was mere inches away from mud.

My breath came in harsh puffs. My knelt position caused her beautiful, wavy hair touch mud, few locks stuck on my soaked shirt. Water dripped from her hair and mixed in mud. I sent a quick prayer to God that I didn't fail. A nauseating sound caused my head to snap towards the source only to to find Troy throw a punch or two at the moron real hard.

I swathe my hands around the girl cautiously and picked her up, surprisingly she weighed nothing! "Take care of this, I will be back soon," were my last words before I jogged towards Medic tent.

My steps were big as I almost darted towards the tent. All I knew I had to get the girl somewhere away from rain somewhere safe. Her body trembled uncontrollably, a sign of grave fever. Without any warning I barged in the tent, which a male soldiers should not do, because at this hour only female doctors used it and sometimes rested here as well.

My eyes fell upon Fiona, the only female doctor I knew. She was a good friend of mine. She left her bed and came towards me with extreme concern in her eyes. "Here," Fiona pointed towards the bed which was empty.

I lay the girls body tenderly on the center and covered her form with a quilt. Under the light I got to see her clearly. She was pallid, very pale. Her lips had transformed in to an awful shade of purple, the bruises on cheek and forehead were fresh with warm blood.

Did the moron hurt her?

"What happened to her?" Fiona interrogated, and engaged herself with the nursing while I stood there like a moron.

"I don't know-just-just take care of her. I have some unfinished business to do," with that I turned my back on them and went back to where I had left Lee. I wasn't astonished to find they were still there. Troy trashed against Chase's grip and Lee grinned like the idiot he was.

I growled and snatched Lee by his t-shirt, balled my fists and landed a solid face-breaking punch to his nose. Blood splashed all over his face. I let go of shirt and he fell on mud, I disregarded the fact that dirt had covered half of my form I delivered another punch which turned his head to the side.

"Scums like you are worth dying. How could you do this? Huh? We are supposed to protect not destroy," I bellowed, my fist slammed his jaw. Strong arms yanked me off of Lee and shoved my body back. I stumbled but stood to my ground.

Lee stayed there for a few good seconds, just lay there breathing fast and not moving, then he pushed himself up and climbed to his feet. "You will pay, you son of a _," he growled and wiped blood off his mouth. I made to pounce at him again, but Troy grabbed my writs and pushed me back with force.

"That's enough! He has had enough. Let Colonel handle this spineless swine," Troy reminded. I ignored his order and launched myself at the prick again, pushed Troy aside when he made to grab my hands again.

Only inches away from him I glared down in Lee's eyes. He was wasted but a glint of terror gleamed in his eyes just for a splint second. I tightened my hands around the fabric of his t-shirt. "I will make sure that you kiss you Medal good bye, and I will make sure you don't get you see another day in this Base or in Military. That's a promise," I snarled in a low deep voice.

I can't do that, but then again I have another card to play. My father's name and his status, even though I don't desire to be in his shadow, but I have to and I want to. I know if I did, this pig won't last long, and that's exactly what I wanted.

There was a long glaring session between me and Lee then I pushed him back and turned to find out what happened to that girl.

I went back in the tent to see Fiona, she examined the IV on the girl's right hand. "How is she doing?" I demanded and stood few inches away from her bed.

"She has a high fever, and I still haven't checked her wounds, they could have gotten infected," Fiona replied, she grabbed a towel in order to dry the girl's hair.

I was certain Troy has already apprised Colonel about this unfortunate occurrence by now and there was a lot of elucidating to do.

"Can you please tell me what happened to this girl?" She asked in a light, sympathetic voice.

"Not now. I can't tell you, but soon I will." I promised, and stared at the unconscious girl. The sight of her twisted something inside of me. I recalled what had happened to her hours ago, wasn't that enough that she had to go through this shit as well?

"Fiona you take good care of her. I will check on you guys later first I have to talk to the Colonel." I told her and departed from the tent again. The moment I was out of the tent Troy cam in view knackered and immensely enraged. It still rained and our rest had long gone to shoved itself up a cow's ass!

"Where are you going?" He questioned when he matched my footsteps.

"Back to the Base to pour out explanation." I quickened my pace.

"No need, he is already here." Troy filled in.

I halted on my spot and rotated to face him. "You informed him."

"The moment you left." He replied with a nod.

"Where is he?" I inquired, wiped the water from my head.

"The tent we were supposed to get some damn rest an hour ago." He snapped. I nodded and turned to strode back to the tent where this all started! This was not going to be pleasant I could feel it. But no matter what they say I will do everything in my power to kick Lee's ass out of army.

That's my word.

Chapter 6

All these years of my life people categorized me as the man who would communicate with his fists instead of his mouth, overprotective, and truculent. That I would never back down from a brawl and shield the ones I cherish. It was I who had shown stars to Maximus when he attempted to touch my sister, Maya.

And today it was the same thing all over again. I struck the hell out of Lee because of a girl I wasn't acquainted with. Something about the way she had peered at me when we'd saved her caused me to do this. She had just lost her entire family. This shouldn't have happened to her especially not today.

We marched towards the tent where Colonel waited for us, with onerous steps. There was a fierce hurricane of thoughts in my brain. My fists curled into balls as a sight flashed before my eyes.

"His face-" I trailed off unable to finish my sentence and rubbed my chin. Troy looked at me and sighed.

"His face will haunt her," he completed my sentence.

Promptly something went off in my brain and I turned to the other side and took a step, "Hey man, where are you going?" Troy called.

"The thing I vowed to Lee," I looked over my shoulder at him. "Troy, I want you to unfold everything to Colonel. I will see you in five," I vocalized, then patted him on his shoulder and once again turned around to depart.

It wasn't strenuous to spot Lee. I saw him crouched behind a few wild bushes, with his head bowed. I strolled up to him and grabbed his collar, hauling him up from the mud he sat on. "What the-" he stopped when I shook his body.

"You don't get to say anything. It's a shame that you are a soldier on the same field as I am. I suggest you don't utter anything or I will ruin you," I warned in a dangerous tone that shut him up for good. I was well aware Troy was already there in the tent so it was my duty to escort Lee there. Trust me I had no intentions whatsoever of performing the task with courtesy.

"Let go, Blade. I ain't your slave. You can't just kick me out of here they can ignore this because we all know we need soldiers," Lee snarled when I dragged him towards the tent. Once again I spun around on my heels to face him, eye-to-eye.

"I suggest you keep those lips of yours sealed before I cut them," no matter how much I detested it but he did have a point. They assassinated our men with the hours that passed and we needed everyone, then again what he committed cannot be pardoned, he has to be condemned for his sinful behavior.

The glare on my face brought a frown to him, "Pray, Lee, pray that they will have mercy on you and if I am lucky and they do let you go. Then It will be my duty to destroy every day of your life, because I despise you with every fiber in my being," without another word I dragged him again like a hound.

Sun was up and radiant refugees strolled out of their tents, tranquil. When their eyes fell on us, they provided me with peculiar and addled looks. However, I disregarded them. Zach, our squad leader walked towards Colonel's tent as well, he raised an eyebrow when he saw us.

"What is going on?" Zach demanded in a stern tone.

"Nothing important, Sir," I passed him and entered the tent. Instantly I freed my fingers from Lee's collar like it scorched my skin. Then saluted and stood at attention, next to Troy. Lee's salute swayed as the effect of alcohol lingered in his body like a specter.

"How did this happen?" Colonel interrogated in a furious low voice. I stood in attention, and looked over his head, grateful that my eyes were not on his face right now. But soon I had to when Colonel ordered. "At ease,"

I separated my feet twelve inches, eased my body a little bit, and looked Colonel straight in the eyes. His eyes sifted to Troy.

"How did you find the girl?" investigated James Black. I elucidated what had occurred an hour ago, the things they needed to know, of course, I excluded the part where I made Lee my punching bag. Their expressions changed from disbelief to perplexity, from revolt to fury, and ceased there.

"And where is the victim now?" Lieutenant questioned darkly.

"In the medic tent, sir. The victim's state is not well, high fever and many serious injuries." I informed

"Was there anyone else who witnessed this?" Lieutenant demanded from Troy.

"Yes sir, Private Chase was present at the scene before we arrived," Troy apprised him.

"No one else? None of the refugees?" Colonel asked, resting his elbow on the table in front of him.

"Not sure sir, we didn't see anyone," Troy replied.

"This event cannot be divulged to the public. Those refugees are under our protection and this accident will ignite unwanted apprehension in their hearts," Colonel growled, looking at Chase and then at the man who stood next to me.

The colonel rose from his chair and advanced in Lee's direction, like a Lion who stalked his prey. Colonel James Black stood inches away from Lee.

"Explain, and you better have a good justification soldier," he hissed in a voice that Lee shivered. It was extremely hushed in here for a few good seconds then it came. "Don't you dare look down," barked James at Lee. "Answer me! Tell me why did you do this? Why have you broken my rules?"

I didn't move my gaze from the spot I stared at.

"I_I was patrolling and-"Lee trailed off.

"And what?" pressed Colonel with a yell.

Lee orated the tale of how he had captured her. At first, I didn't care but when he mentioned how she had been wandering alone in the night and how brutally he had caught her. That did it for me, It was enough to wake the wrath inside my chest. The pig even dared enough to explain 'in detail' how he had approached her, and how the girl screamed for help.

"Her yell had demanded attention, that's when Private Chase and the others found us," Lee explained, his eyes did not look elsewhere but in James's eyes and I knew, hell I knew it was daunting to look in them. His gaze was like lightning, that shred every ounce of courage in Lee's heart.

James inhaled in an attempt to calm himself. "You took benefit of the refugees my men risked their lives to save. You drank while on duty knowing well it is forbidden. You broke my rules and were brave enough to threaten my men who had saved the victim from you. You," he stepped forward. "Can kiss you medal goodbye and will be spending good days behind bars in an attempt of rape and breaking military rules," Colonel growled, after a few seconds he took a step back from Lee.

"But_" Lee tried to protest.

James rotated around and gave him a deadly glare. "That's enough I won't be hearing any crap from you anymore!" and bellowed in Lee's face. I was glad but certainly not contented.

"Inform Zach to get in here," Colonel told us as he walked back to his chair.

"Roger that sir,"

"Dismissed," Lieutenant ordered. With that, we all departed from the tent, without Lee who was ordered to stay behind. None of us vocalized a word for a while when we stopped a few feet away from Colonel's tent. "Remind me to never piss James off," sighed Chase, Troy chuckled at this.

"You guys going back to the city again?" Chase asked us.

"Yes we have to," I replied downhearted and looked at him closely. He seemed unhinged and looked like he had something to say.

"I don't get it, how can this happen? I mean Lee worshipped his job, serving his country was everything to him. I don't get it," Chase mumbled loud enough for us to hear. Troy glanced at me with a questioning look in his eyes.

"What are you referring to?" he voiced my thoughts, I frowned.

"Lee dreamt about being a soldier, he was my buddy in high school and I knew him too well to go and mess his life up. It's just I don't know why! "Chase answered then pursed his lips.

"That's what happens when you drink. If you commit crimes you will regret your entire damned life. Just a few minutes of fun aren't worth it," I told him sternly. Chase gaped at me for a few seconds then nodded in agreement.

"Anyway I have to go," he gave Troy's shoulder a pat. "We have a mission to do. See you around." with that, he walked away.

Once the sun peeked over the mountains and wind danced around the tents, my body triggered exhaustion in every cell and the mountain of thoughts drained my energy. The mere repulsive thought of what Lee did almost made me turn back around and kill that moron, but unfortunately, I couldn't.

We gradually made our way to the medic tent and I hoped the girl would be fine after what she had been through.

"Is she going to be alright?" Just like earlier, Troy voiced my thoughts again.

I sighed deeply "I doubt it, but I hope so," he gave a nod.

"We still have no idea if we are going back or something else has been decided. Why don't you check on her while I ask Zach what they have decided," Troy said, took off his cap rubbed his head with his left hand then wore it back on.

"Okay, I will catch up with you," I told him, he gave a short nod and marched away.

As soon as I stepped into the tent smell of medicine hit my nostrils hard and my muscles relaxed in the warm atmosphere. I sauntered forward and saw that almost all the patients were asleep except for one.

She was awake.

The girl was awake. She sat there, her legs folded up on the bed to her chest and her head rested on her knees, with her arms enveloped around them. I started to walk up to her slowly but halted dead on my track when she raised her head at my approach. Tears rushed down those green eyes and glistered on her cheeks.

I was well aware she was terrified but I didn't want her to be afraid of me. There were bandages on her hands and another on her forehead, blood ran through the IV on her right hand. She hugged the covers to her chest and gulped when I stepped closer and stood a foot away from her bed.

And then, it happened swiftly I had no time to register it. One second she gaped at me with those despaired and desperate eyes, the other second they turned to agitation and horror. I watched her carefully and saw her breathing speed up and uneasiness took over her. She started to back away from me.

"It's okay. I am not going to hurt you," I assured her as gently as I could manage. To make it more convincing I raised my hands in the air, but she didn't listen as more salty tears trickled down those eyes. I observed as they rolled down her cheeks to her throat Then a sob escaped her lips and that made me frown.

"Shh...calm down_" before I could finish, her sobs became loud and she sank deeper into the covers, eyes wide and she backed a little further. Fear took over her form in a bat of an eye.

The girl was about to fall from the bed that's when I closed the distance between me and the bed and stretched my hand to wrap my fingers around her arm, not knowing that it was an unintelligent move.

She screamed and threw her legs over the other side of the bed then turned around to escape from me. I ignored her constant yells which had woken up almost all the patients. I walked around the bed where she stood, her hand that quivered seized the footboard for support.

I gritted my teeth as rage started to ascend within me. How can she not know the difference between me and Lee? I was the one who saved her from the catastrophe fate!

"You need to calm down, ma'am. I am not here to hurt you," I repeated, and inched closer to her. She stepped back and a whimper reached my ears. Instantly she looked around to find a way to flee, but I wasn't going to let that happen. She was not in a state to be out of bed, she needs rest.

Why can't she get it? Why can't she understand that I am trying to help her?

Before she took another step, I encased my hands around her middle, with her back to my chest, pulled her up a foot or two from the floor, and twisted our bodies towards the bed. The girl yelled and pushed harder on my arms to free her fragile body from my cage.

"Will you stop it?" I hissed, dumbstruck at her actions. Why the hell is she acting like this?

"What is going on here?" Fiona rushed towards us.

I Ignored her, lifted the girl once again very gently, and put her tiny form on the bed. Before I could remove my hands she wrapped the covers over her body. I scowled and moved backward. Fiona repeated her question, this time more harshly.

"I_I don't know, Fiona," I sighed, " You know I wouldn't dream of doing anything bad to her," I blurted out. She pushed my shoulder and walked passed me and placed her hand on the girl's shoulder, who at once wrapped her trembling hands around 'The doctor'.

"It's okay, he will never hurt you. I promise," Fiona cooed, as I stared at them, staggered.

"Blade, she is horrified and you scared her even more," Fiona snapped desperately with an edge of vexation in her tone. She rested her palm on my wet shirt and gently shoved me backward. "Go," I did not move. "Please, she needs rest,"

"But I won't hurt her," I protested, with a jerk of my hand towards the feeble girl, who wept, then buried her face in Fiona's jacket.

"Blade_" Fiona began.

I disregarded her yet once again then sat down on the chair in front of her bed, so close that the fabric of my shirt touched the steel and I looked straight into her eyes. It was exactly the same rush of feelings I had felt the first time when my blue ones met hers. Even though she had been drenched in blood, her hair messy, her face pale. Her innocence screamed out to me, just like it did now.

The girl's sobs died down a little and calmed down in Fiona's presence so I started; "I am not going to harm you, you need to know that," I licked my lip. "Please trust me. No one will touch you. That's a promise," I vowed softly, as her sobs died completely.

She did not look up at me, a tear fell from the corner of her left eye. My heart rolled over at the sight in front of me. No matter the consequences I have to make her trust me.

"Don't be scared, I am the last person on earth you need to fear," I murmured, sincerity dripping from my voice.

To my astonishment, she eventually raised her head up to look at me, and trust me I almost lost myself in her eyes. A frown appeared on my face when she glanced at Fiona and then back at me. When her eyes met mine again, I felt a wave of emotions collided in my heart, something I couldn't comprehend happened at that moment.

Was it sympathy?

"You should leave," Fiona glared at me when I just sat there.

With a nod, I rose to my feet and darted away, furious at what had just happened. On my way back, I couldn't help but kick the chair that sat next to the tent flap. My head throbbed and it reminded me that I needed some darn rest and this made it even worse. I marched away and passed refugees, they backed away instantly just from the enraged look on my face. Then at once I stopped in a mud puddle and inhaled a few deep breaths in order to control myself.

"Blade," called a familiar voice. I looked up to see Troy stare at me intently. "What happened man?"

With a growl, I informed him of everything. He was hushed for a minute as though this was hard to take in. I knew he knew what I thought at that moment. The thing that I despise the most is being misunderstood. It creates undesirable adversities in life.

"You can't blame her, "Troy commented with his positive tone, I barely nodded." She is extremely terrified."

"Yeah man, but we were the ones who saved her." I snapped. He sighed vanquished. We lapsed into silence so server it clawed at my throat. The only sound we heard was the water that tipped from the tents.

"Oh yeah, Zach has been ordered that his team stays back for another day because of what happened and we will get down to business tomorrow," Troy filled in.

"Well, It's better that way we will get some darn rest," I said annoyed.

"Blade, you got to understand and keep your fury aside just for a few seconds pal and think about it, her family was slaughtered, and the poor soul was almost raped." I flinched at the last word. Troy rested his hand on my shoulder and my shoulders sagged a bit.

"I know dude, it's just the way she looked at me made me feel like I am the bloody criminal here," I spat.

"It's not her fault, after what she has experienced of course she will think all men are like that monster," his words did make sense but they weren't any good to me today. For some reason, he couldn't calm me down. However, I nodded and attempted to terminate the conversation there and then.

He smiled.

"You know man, you did well with that pig today," memories of Lee's bleeding face flashed in my brain, and I grinned.

"You were always the one who had the most fun in life," Troy kept on going, his lips twitched. I raised an eyebrow, well aware of where he was going. "Come on man I am serious, you beat the hell out of Maximus, and man that was fun to watch, wonder how it felt, and today you almost toasted Lee."

I chuckled silently. "I can't deny that sure was fun, you should try it sometimes. Aaa! Wait, you ain't the one who favors fights. Right?" I teased, looking up at the sky as the sun climbed the stairs slowly.

"You want to count the number of fights I was in?" he demanded then crossed his hands over his chest.

"No man, we know your past and know this as well that it was you who taught me how to punch in kinder garden," he laughed at this and shook his head at the memory.

"You got a solid point there," Troy beamed, satisfied and we fist-bumped.

Troy has been my friend ever since I can remember. Where I was the boy who had everything in life on the other hand his life was a disaster. His optimism was always there and that kept his going on in life. I would beat the hell out of anyone who dared go against him, and he would only try and communicate to them. There are times I wondered how we became friends, but I remember it.

Remember the day when we were young and some big bullies kicked my butt, well not literally. It was my culpability for calling their captain "Fat " Troy had saved me by calling the teachers and then we had conversed for the first time in life and he had taught me how to make a fist and swing it.

From that day on, I had his back while he did my homework. When I decided to walk on the footsteps of my father and become a soldier. Troy had sweltering wrath in his heart because of his brother so he acceded to join the army.

And today, here we are, ready to die for each other. And trust me I won't think twice before throwing myself in front of death for him because once he had done the same for me.

Chapter 7

Even though the bed was smaller for my huge size, the comfort and luxury it gifted were wondrous. My body yearned for more rest and my head howled to rest on a soft pillow. It has been six hours since Troy and I rested while others in our team were...I don't know what they were doing because I was sleeping.

I rubbed my hands down my face and yawned like a pathetic lion. My eyes tingled a little from lack of sleep. I sat straight and looked around the tent with my right eye shut. There were only a few soldiers who rested on their bunk beds. I was sure they had just returned from their arduous and wearisome missions. I looked up at the weight on the bed on top of mine, which indicated Troy was still asleep.

I yawned like a bear again and cranked my neck. Threw my legs over the bed and stood up to my full height. Now that I stood I rubbed my neck and stared at Troy lying there. His right leg dangled from the side of the bed and he snored like he freaking owned this place. I glanced at my watch to find out it was 14:00 pm.

"Troy I am off to take a shower, rest time is about to end," I shook his body like always because my voice wasn't enough to wake him up.

He grunted in response and I took that as a sign to leave the tent. Sunshine hit my eyes and I blinked a few times to adjust the light. The world was already up, soldiers moved around getting ready to depart. Somehow it reminded me of ants how they scurried around and followed what their queen had ordered them, but we did not have queens here, more like big fearless bulls.

We had returned back to Base after the little scene with the girl. Troy and I were ordered to get some slumber and trust me, I almost dashed to bed. Every limb in my form was in agony and entreated for some well-earned rest.

Once I was done with the shower I literally kicked Troy so that he would wake up. I hung my rifle over my shoulder and left the tent to meet Zach. On my way there to locate our team leader I saw Carlos, who smiled up at me, "Good morning," he teased.

"Afternoon," I kept walking, " What are you up to?" I asked him.

"Just following orders. Are you going to see Zach?" Carlos asked once he matched my footsteps. I responded with a nod. "He left for the refugee camp with Colonel an hour ago, don't ask me why. Seems like something is up," he said, interested.

"Okay," I told him with a slight frown. Why was Zach there and with Colonel? "When exactly are we leaving?" I questioned him, as we turned around a corner.

"After about two hours, Zach will be here and then we are off," Carlos informed. I hummed in reply as we stopped and waited for Troy to catch up with us. After fifteen minutes, he arrived and we made our way towards the refugee camp, while Carlos stayed behind to follow the orders he was given.

"Why did Colonel and Zach go to meet her?" Troy inquired.

I glanced at him sideways. "Zach was involved because we, his team comrades were the ones who kicked Lee's backside, so it was wise to let him know why his team stayed behind for another day instead of moving. As for Colonel, I think he went to be certain the girl is fine," I told him the same thing I had been thinking since Carlos filled in.

"We have an hour left before moving. I want to find out what happened there since we left," Troy said and inched his rifle closer to his chest.

We sauntered into the camp, refugees were engaged in their daily life activities. Children who had no idea their lives were destroyed played around the tents, some even played in the mud puddles caused by the furious rain. Troy ruffled a young boy's hair who darted past him in a tent.

It was obvious we all like children so did Troy. He cared too much for him, so much that his death had shattered Troy into pieces. By him, I mean Troy's younger brother, Nicolas. He was murdered by some tugs at the age of six.

We were only seventeen years old, and that day Nicolas had desired to come along with us to play basketball. With Troy's big heart he couldn't say no. Just like every other day our friends divided into groups and started playing while Nicolas sat on a bench and cheered for his brother who was my opponent.

Suddenly like an uninvited guest, fireworks pierced the air, and shock, and agitation spread in our bodies. Time had stilled as I just stood for the bullets to shower on us. Other boys endeavored to escape and I searched around for Troy, disregarding that very moment someone has pointed his gun at me and fired before the bullet could pierce my skin. I was shoved back with force and my head had hit the cement ground hard.

Troy was the one who had propelled me, his body fell on top of mine to prevent himself from getting shot. Everything had gone silent, hearing gunshots back then was the most terrifying thing I had ever experienced. I couldn't shake the fear that had swelled in my body for a few good minutes.

Troy had then pushed himself off of me and ran for someone. I remember I winced at the pain in my skill but sat up, only to see Troy squatting over someone.

That was the moment I regret the most in my life. Nicolas drenched in blood had changed the serene look in Troy's eyes into a rage and unfathomable pain. What was worse his older brother had left Troy and his mother after two days after Nick's funeral. Troy was mentally tormented and that was when I decided to make a decision. After only five months I turned eighteen and stepped on the path my father had made and Troy had agreed. Because the raging wrath in his heart would have led him to commit crimes he knew he would regret in life.

I shook myself from the past as we kept walking towards the medic tent.

"Seems like you remembered something from the past," Troy commented.

I gave him a muddled look as we neared the tent. "How do you?" I conceded.

"There is always a look on your face when you remember a memory," he enunciated. I chuckled at him. Damn him and his skills of knowing me so well.

We walked into the tent and at once spotted Colonel, he sat on the chair I had sat on hours ago and Zach stood a few feet away from him. Troy and I halted where Zach stood. He looked at us with hoisted eyebrows and we simply give him a quick nod, then looked back at Colonel.

He had the girl's small, frail hand in his huge one and rubbed circles on the pale skin. The man knew how to tackle demoralized girls because of his own daughter. Colonel conversed in a hushed voice, I was not at all interested in his words, I stared at the girl. I didn't see her utter a word, she merely stared at him.

"Do you think she is mute?" Troy whispered after what felt like an eternity. I gave him a "Are you serious" look. He shrugged. "Look at her, she is not saying a word, all she does is give short nods," he murmured. A deep frown made its way to my face.

Come to think of it, since we have saved her, the girl has not spoken a word. She had only screamed. A lump burned my throat and I licked my lips. Suddenly I felt exceedingly apprehensive, there were sentiments I didn't comprehend and they pissed me off. She cannot be mute!

I polished off the frown from my face when Fiona looked at us. She rolled her eyes and marched where we stood. Here we go!

"What are you two doing here? The colonel said no one is to come here," she whisper yelled. Troy grinned at her. I knew he was going to fire one of his comebacks in front of Zach, so I cut in.

"We were here to make sure the patient is well," I said, grabbed Troy's arm, and dragged him a few feet away from them.

"What was that?"

"I don't want to be kicked out of here," he clenched his jaw at me but did not vocalize another word.

I observed as Colonel talked to her for a long time and her lips didn't move. The girl really couldn't talk! It made me furious more than it should. She could be aphonic, there are chances for that, it is usually caused by an injury or illness but she can't be mute!

I had to make sure the girl is not mute before I leave this place.

When Colonel was done with the conversation he gave the girl's shoulder a pat, a tender fatherly pat, and walked back to Zach, who saluted for him and followed Colonel towards the tent flap. They ceased their movement when he saw us. We saluted him and greeted him an 'Afternoon'

"What are you two doing here soldiers?" He demanded.

"Checking on the patient, sir," I responded, my body stiff in attention.

"The girl is fine. Move soldiers, your team goes in one hour!" he commanded harshly, all the softness I had witnessed a minute ago evaporated.

I watched them leave the tent, sure I would obey his orders but not before I do what I had planned. I walked to the bed, where she sat, head bowed. I was anxious she might start screaming again. Troy followed close behind me I knew he thought the same thing, that we might frighten her.

When we stopped at her bed, both Fiona and the girl with green eyes looked up at us, her eyes went wide and Fiona glared at us.

"I am here to make sure she is okay," I spoke and pushed my rifle behind my back to hide it from view.

"As you can see she is extremely fine," Fiona argued.

"We want to hear that from the girl we saved," Troy butt in. Fiona exhaled melodramatically.

I looked down at her and passed a very small smile. I had no freaking intentions of terrifying the crap out of her. The girl was in clean, fresh clothes. The light blue cotton gown was loose, and her glossy brown hair cascaded down her left shoulder. She wasn't that pallid and the cut on her lip was better.

"I just wanted to make sure you are fine?" I announced eyes on her. There were no emotions at all. I needed her to say something, anything to make sure she was not mute. I had to prove Troy was wrong and this girl could talk. She gave a nod and dropped her gaze, just like that. Not even a single emotion crossed her eyes. And she didn't talk.

She couldn't speak!

I grit my teeth and stepped back to get the hell out of that place. I didn't understand why it vexed me that much, it was not at all okay with me that she couldn't speak. Was I hurt? Did I feel bad she couldn't communicate?

When we departed from the refugee camp, we had settled in a Hummer Humvee. Zach was apprised that our mission was to ambush a group of terrorists not far from here. Two teams were designated for this hazardous mission, ours and another. We all knew this shit was perilous, during the time we were here, we had come to learn that our enemies were highly trained and had the same skills that we possessed and developed over years.

This war was not just a terrorist attack, it was deeper. Their main purpose was to demolish West and make the government kiss their feet. One thing they were not aware of was that they had to go through us in order to achieve what they desired.

Edginess was dense in our Humvee. Our squad was the third team they sent to terminate those monsters and it was also to see if we will succeed because none of the soldiers before us had returned back from this mission. That was the reason every member felt furious. We were to drive and patrol, without raising alarm, and attack if possible ambush. We required luck, a whole lot of luck, to get there and get this over with.

I sat in the back of the Humvee, with my head leaned back and eyes closed. I thought about my sister. Man I missed her so much. An elbow nudged my hand and I opened my eyes to look at Mason.

"We are here," he announced and wore his helmet. I copied his moves as the back door opened. We soldiers stepped out of the Humvee. Zach, who drove got out with his rifle drawn, and Troy, who sat in the passenger seat, came to stand with us. We looked around for peril, waited for Zach's orders and they were given after few seconds.

Our team shadowed Zach who led us to a wall of a building; I couldn't really guess what the building was, through all that blood smeared on it. The weather was not with us today, it was windy. The wind after a while engulfed us in a small hurricane of its own.

Zach signalled with hand signal for us to move. Troy, Mason and I parted from the group and proceeded towards the right side where another building stood. We drew our guns and looked out for danger. So far nothing, deserted street. Enraged wind blew rapidly and took dust particles with it. I glanced over at Zach, who was on the left side of the street, backed against a wall, almost twenty feet away from us.

I was the one who led the two men behind me, but not before I consulted matters with Zach. I could literally hear the tortured screams of our men who were assassinate here, a brutal, ruthless death. Their audacity haunted this street like a phantom, and the shadows of their souls touched us.

The faded sound of their guns that had once blazed reached my ears and my heart commenced to beat fast, not from terror, but from pure passion to eliminate souls and extreme perturbation.

"Lets saddle up boys," hollered Zach through the radio and we charged.

Chapter 8

F ive days crawled by in severe trepidation. We had been patrolling in the Humvee ever since then. This place was hazardous, and my bum hurt like hell from all the sitting in the back. Those scoundrels had planted mines near their hideouts, which made it almost insurmountable for us to march in and annihilate them. The place we were in, was supposedly a town that was now owned by these monsters after they slaughtered all the residents.

Our team was exhausted after all the killing that went along with the fading sun. The men in my team were wounded but it wasn't grievous. Zach would calculate the times we were ambushed and would think of a new strategy to move around like shadows. It was devastating and intolerable, rest hours were the same, two of us would look out for about two and a half hours.

Rest was eminently important for us, without it our bodies would not function in a proper manner even when orders were yelled at us. Right now it was 1:00 in the morning, my man Mason and I had the duty to the lookout. My team rested in a room that had no roof and was torn apart. It was supposed to be a house I guess a Bazooka didn't like its design.

Well, I suppose it was preferable to sleeping under the open, vast sky or on sticky, cold dirt. Mason and I were outside the room and literally kicked ourselves to remain awake. I got wearied of standing motionless so I hopped on the bonnet of the Humvee, with my rifle in hand and looked skywards. The stars glistered like tiny diamonds and the crescent smiled down on us puny humans. It got chillier and bitter day by day as winter knocking at the door.

I heard footsteps and rotated my head to my right only to find Mason. He strolled to where I sat. "What's up?" he asked, then mirrored my posture and sat beside me.

"Nothing just looking at the stars," I murmured the truth.

"Damn," he chuckled, "Now that would have been bizarre if you said you were making a wish," he joked which made us both laugh.

"Nah I can't wish upon a star I am a few million years late," Mason turned to look at me with a raised brow, " The star is already dead," his other brow lifted, "According to astronomy," here his lips twitched and he guffawed.

The silence was what followed us after that. "Just half an hour then we can rest," I sighed, and rubbed my neck.

"Man, I am tired," he complained, looking around at the gloomy world around us.

"Yo Mase, did you talk to Angelic?" I glanced at him sideways.

A dejected smile appeared on his lips. "Yeah back at the Base I did, and to Tasha as well, even though all she did was babble," he chuckled at the mention of his baby girl.

"It's been forever since I visited, last time I saw Tasha she was just five months old," I told him as I recalled the day I held his baby girl in my hands. Man, Tasha looked exactly like her mother, Angelic, they both were really heavenly.

"She is almost a year old now," Mason smiled. I grinned back at him.

Mason loved Angelic ever since he had seen her in high school. Yeah, she was voluptuous, I agree and every man desired her. Mase was after her for a long time and in the end, she fell for him once he materialized in front of her in the army uniform. She could not help but say 'yes' when he proposed to her.

Mase had been my buddy since Army college. I liked his disposition, he didn't give a crap about the world and just did what he thought was right. He is now the Doc of our team, an unimpeachable friend, and a virtuous man.

"Why was our team delayed for a day?" Mase interrogated me and brought my attention back to him. His blue eyes zeroed on me. I pursed my lips and unfolded everything, he was my man, my teammate who saved the girl.

The one I could not stop thinking about.

"Holy shit! All that happened and I had no idea," he growled as anger took control.

I nodded. "As for Lee, he is behind bars enjoying his time," I informed him with a smirk.

He narrowed his eyebrows. "Did Marshal know about this?"

"Colonel apprised him and I made sure he used his mastery to get Lee behind the bars," I said boastfully. Mase seemed appeased.

After a while he began again; "Poor soul, that pimp shouldn't have done that," I didn't utter anything as my thoughts lingered back to the girl with green eyes.

The thought that she could not talk pained me. I was perplexed as to why I couldn't stop thinking about her? Every hour her enchanting eyes displayed in my brain and I couldn't help but to wish I could see her again. I guess I was protective of her. Protective of my refugee, but then again why only her? I have saved so many people that I lost count of them years ago then why can't I stop thinking about her?

"I'll go around and check the back," Mase jumped off the Humvee hood and walked away. I sighed.

"Loading," Zach yelled over the guns that wailed, instantly we covered him and fired at the enemy.

Our drive around this area at the dawn was treacherous and we were under attack. The attack was unpredictable. We abandoned the Humvee and my team sheltered behind walls which were our only protection from the enemy

I stood in the hurricane of death and fired at the terrorists. This act only thrust my anger meter to a hundred percent. These monsters were like dark shadows in the night, so near yet impossible to locate. They were vigorous, very tough. The only thing my brain reasoned right now was, to hell with being killed I have to kill.

"Grenades," Zach screamed.

Bruce on my right snatched two grenades, pulled the safety pin and flung them as far as he could, while Mason stood almost fifty feet ahead of us, he covered his body behind a car and emptied his rifle.

Beads of perspiration streamed down my forehead and fell on my eyelashes. The salty liquid stung my eyes. I fluttered my eyes to make my vision clear, and tightened my grip on my rifle. Every member yelled orders or warned the others, but I only heard one.

"Soldier down! Soldier down! " hollered Zach's voice.

I stiffened on my root as a chill snaked down my spine. Promptly I twisted my head so fast that it almost cracked, to see if Troy was alright, to see if Troy was alive. There he stood, alive, breathing but then who?

I trailed Troy's gaze where he stared, shock and terror perceptible on his ashen face. Then we saw as our friend's body collapsed on the ground, pale and cold. Mason was drenched in his own blood, the car was the only thing that shielded his body from the bullets that were showered on him.

"PULL BACK!" Zach screamed. "I REPEAT PULL THE HELL BACK!" to all of us. I shook myself from the trance and gaped at Zach.

"What do you mean?" I barked at him as he took down a terrorist.

"We have to get the hell out of here, get in the damn Humvee. Those are orders," he bellowed back over the guns and did not spare me a glance. Zach, our mighty and ferocious leader killed his targets. I looked at Mason's body then back at our team leader who like a Lion pounced on his enemy but not with his claws, with his rifle.

I glared at him, ducked down at the right moment as a bullet pierced the wall inches away from my head, cement dust hit my face. "What about Mason's body?" I shouted, ceased my firing only to look at him.

"Are you kidding me? If we go there, then we all are dead," Zach barked the words loud and clear. He expected me to dig a grave in my brain and bury his orders there.

Screw his rules.

"I am not leaving without his body," was my enraged response. Zach turned to me, a maniac, incensed look in his eyes, his huge chest rose and fell from him rapid breathing. We glared at each other just for a split second, and in that second I challenged my caption, my team leader to try and prevent me. After all I was my father's son.

"I will not risk my soldiers."

Bloody oaf.

"What will you tell his family, that you got him murdered and were not able to get them his corpse back. I have seen him gaze at his wife's picture, what will you give her? Huh? " I hollered, fury flared in my veins.

"These are my bloody orders!" Zach bawled in my face, and shoved me against the wall. He protected us from the bullets that made their way towards us.

Son of a!

"I am going there," I pointed where Mason's body lay benumb fifty feet away. "And I am bringing his body here. If you want to cover me you are welcome captain, if not, go screw yourself," I roared these words, reloaded my rifle, spared a glance at Troy who gaped at me like I was freaking deranged.

With that I leaped in the scene.

If you question why I was being a blockhead, the only reply I would be able to provide you is his wife and his daughter. I cannot let them bury nothing but a casket in his commemoration. They deserved better, Mason died for his country, this was the least I could do for him.

Yes I was threw myself in front of guns, that blazed from every direction. Yes, I knew that there were ninety nine point nine percent of chances that I would be dead before I got to Mason's body. But I had to try.

I drew my rifle higher and started shooting towards my enemy, who stood behind cars or windows. It was hard for me to dart with all the weight I carried, my combat boots made prints on earth as I dodged a pile of dirt.

May God help my soul! Bullets whizzed by me and barely missed my body. However, that didn't stop me. I marched forward and terminated the monsters.

Suddenly my body was pushed aside with force, and my back collided with a wall. I looked up only to see a very inceansed Troy standing in front of me. "What the hell were you thinking?" He shrieked , then shoved me harder against the wall in rage.

"Thanks for coming," I gasped and faked a smirk as my throat went dry.

"I am going to whip the hell out of you once we get the hell out of here," he barked in my ear, then reloaded his gun. "Go, get his body, I got you covered," I wanted to grin but that exact moment the earth trembled beneath my feet and a huge voice sliced the air.

Once again we played with death. Troy fired wherever he spotted a target, so did I. I knew well enough that Zach and the others were helping us out. And I think I will express my gratitude when I return. That is IF we get back!

My heart started to beat rapidly and run against time, gooseflesh appeared on my arm from utter fright. Mason's body was just a few feet away from us. Adrenaline pumped in my veins, sweat trickled down my head then mingled with dirt and blood on my face which were caused from my wounds.

A yell resulting from severe fury escaped my lips whenever my bullet pierced a skull or ripped their hearts. I knew they killed for delectation, I annihilated them for revenge. They desired and searched power in it, I on the other hand learned pain and remorse from it.

Three feet away.

Bullets almost hit my shoes, but I didn't stop. Troy backed me up with everything he got. I used all my training and bent down, seized the back of Mason's bulletproof, and hauled his body. I threw it over my shoulder and darted back to where we came from. Troy hot on my heels, every now and then Troy would lift his rifle and fire.

Mason's body weighed but I didn't pay much heed to it. We had to get the hell out of there as soon as possible. The wall Troy had pushed me against was only a few feet away.

Come on, Come on faster faster! I pleaded in my brain.

My grip was firm on his body, and it tightened when I stumbled. A skull ripping pain shot up my right arm, and crimson blood oozed from it. I was shot, shot in my hand. Just like every time I disregarded the pain and turned the corner then hid behind the wall for my life. Time moved fast with our lives at stake.

My breath came out in heavy puffs, I lay Mason's body and peered at the bullet that cut deep in my arm. The damned bullet had carved a deep hole in my bicep. I gritted my teeth at the inflaming sensation in my arm, water burned in my eyes, my pulse hammered against my chest. It wasn't the blood, it wasn't the pain that urged me to bang my head against the wall, it was the freaking fear and desperation of getting the hell out of this place.

"You idiot, I swear Blade, you are insane," Troy yelled, pressed like a gum on the wall next to me on my left side.

"We have to move!" I bellowed once again, threw Mason's body over my shoulder then hissed at the severe throbbing. We dashed towards the rest of the group, once again our attempt was to ignore the bullets that pierced the fragile air. I disregarded the damned bullet that cut deeper in my flesh, and the blood that dripped down my arm on the earth.

Three feet.

Two feet.

One!

Zach stepped aside and backed us up, my chest heaved up and down from lack of energy. Instantly I lay Mason's body on the ground and it ripped my heart to see him drenched in blood, his face was colourless, just like a spectre. His eyes were closed and I could swear there was a slight twitch on his lips. Before I could grab my rifle and resume with my duty. I was snatched by my suit shirt in a maniac way, and punched in the jaw.

What the_?

I clenched my jaw and glared at Zach, "Next time go against my orders, and I will make you blody pay. You show off son of a prick," he bawled in my ear, his hand still on my collar.

Troy stepped between us and pushed Zach backwards, "Sir, we have to MOVE!" with those words they grabbed Mason's body and put it in the Humvee.

I took my position and started to retreat slowly. There was no time for me to react on what Zach said, no time to even feel enraged about it. I stole some time for my team to settle in the Humvee, and pulled the trigger whenever I saw the enemy. When my team was set to depart then I spun around and threw myself in, doors were closed right when I dragged my feet in and Zach drove the hell out of there.

There was dense and intense layer of tension in the vehicle. Mainly because we lost one brilliant, tough soldier from our team.

Mason's death was like a gloomy cloud on us, every member grieved for him, and to top it off. I went against Zach's bloody orders.

I sat in silence, my rifle that hand blood stains stood in between my feet, after a moment I bowed my head in anguish. Troy sat beside me, hushed, like everyone else.

"You are bleeding," he pointed out.

"I am fine," I mumbled head down.

"You are bloody shot, Blade," he growled and leaned closer. I turned my head and glare up at my buddy who had a frown on his face "I am not dead! " and snapped at him, which shut him up for good.

Once again I bowed my head and brushed off the oozing blood.

Chapter 9

I growled and shot a deadly, blood-curdling glare at Fiona who was being mulish as hell. With a firm shake of my head, I made to stand up, but Fiona rested her gloved hands on my shoulders and pushed me back on one of the medic tent's beds instead.

"Blade, you have to allow me to look at this, your wound can get infected," Fiona hissed in a distressed tone. I rolled my eyes at her again and endeavored to stand up. She placed her hands on my chest and shoved my body back harshly.

I was in my flighty, bloody combat suit. My shirt was torn and it stunk of sweat and dry blood. I had my rifle propped securely against the table next to the tiny bed as my shoulder was unable to handle its weight.

"Troy we have to hold him." I frowned at her. "I have to get the bullet out of his arm or else he won't be able to use his hand," Fiona ordered Troy, completely disregarding me. Troy stood there with a grim look, he mourned over Mason's death.

"Fiona let it be, it's a reminder of what happened, " I said stiffly. She glared at me then seized my wounded hand.

I hissed and snarled in pain.

"Blade be realistic, this is ridiculous," she argued desperately, her eyes turning dark as anger simmered further in her blood.

Reluctant I permitted the doctor to clean the blood and put some bandages around my wound. After I was done with the vexatious meeting with Colonel I was sent here. The wound was still bleeding and Fion's hawk-like eyes had seen it and demanded an explanation. I informed her I wanted the bullet to be in my arm just to remind me of the day Mason died.

"I have to go," I rose to my feet for the third time; this time Troy pushed me back.

"Colonel won't like this shit," he narrowed his incensed eyes at me almost daring me. He twisted his head towards our doctor. "Get the damn bullet out Fiona," he spat in his that voice that held authority and would work on anyone else but not on me

A growl broke in my throat, and with a clench of my jaw, I opened my mouth, about to fling a merciless comment at Troy. However, my eyes widened when I saw who stood behind Fiona. She wore a loose cotton tee shirt and loose pants, with a tray of medical supplies in her hands. She stared at me with petrified, wide eyes.

My breath hitched when a pair of alluring green eyes met mine. "You have to allow them to take the bullet out and y-you need to calm down," spoke the most melodic voice I had ever heard. I gaped at her like a doltish soul.

She could talk?

I looked at Fiona with a deranged look and demanded, "She can talk?" Fiona rolled her eyes.

"Of course, she can, now will you please let me look at that," she replied, pointing at the bandages around the wound on my right hand. I simply gave a short nod, the girl with green eyes handed Fiona some cleaning medicine and new bandages.

"She works here?" Troy interrogated, disquiet and amazement observable on his face.

"Yes, her father used to be a doctor," Fiona jabbed a damn cream on my wound, water stung my eyes. "So she has ideas on how to aid patients, and she is brilliant in helping me and other doctors. Today is her second day here," Fiona explained, as she wiped dried blood from my skin

I glanced at the girl on my left as she cut a dressing not looking up. She could talk! A smile shadowed my lips as I stared down at her. Even though I sat on the bed, I was still taller than her form. Damn, she was close, so close that my breath fanned her hair. I could smell her intoxicating scent; it was of roses and rain, a faint smell of roses. My eyes followed the way her hair cascaded down her shoulders and caressed her creamy skin. Oh, crap!

I quickly turned my head and looked at Troy who had his brow lifted with a knowing look in his eyes. 'What' I mouthed, he chuckled.

I sighed, then hissed again as Fiona jabbed the damn thing in my wound to get the bullet out. My skin was almost numb so I couldn't feel much of the agony. Moments later, a ding sound caused me to twist my head and scowl at the bullet drenched in my blood on a small steel tray.

I frowned as Mason's face displayed before my eyes. I inhaled sharply to cease emotions that rose in my chest like a beast.

Coming back from the treacherous mission, our Humvee halted at the Base. Soldiers sprinted towards us and helped take Mason's body out from the vehicle I had been informed to have a meeting with Colonel. An encounter I knew would screw my mood further.

When I made sure the others would take good care of Mason,'s body. I made my way towards his tent.

I sat on a chair across Colonel. We were alone in his tent and his wrath howled at me, yet all he did was to stare at me, with no damn expressions on his face. Like I said before, this man knew how to intimidate anyone. And hell I was terrorized.

"You gambled and jeopardized your squad member's lives in danger by going there to get his body, and you did not follow orders given to you," Colonel begin with a low, deep voice, he leaned back in his chair, not averting his piercing gaze from me.

"Yes sir,"

"And you understand what are the consequences of breaking rules?" he interrogated.

"Yes sir,"

"Very well," Colonel inhaled, "Give me an explanation of your actions, soldier," then demanded, leaned forward to rest his hands under his chin. Here I got infuriated. I have been through shit and now this crap drove me insane.

"Sir, I couldn't forget what you had once told us when this mission started," he cocked his head." That 'I will bring my men back dead ...or alive," I reminded and something flashed in his eyes.

"What you did was risky," he growled.

"Aren't we laying down our life at risk every second we are here, sir?" deadly silence lapsed between us. I then spoke again, "I think it was worth it," my voice held confidence.

"Do not teach me what was worth it or not, you could have got killed and could have gotten all the men killed in the bloody team," he hollered, his eyes glaring straight in mine. " Therefore you will stay here for a month and will patrol on the refugee camp as a punishment of you actions,"

He is got to be shitting me! I froze and subconsciously clenched my fist. A month without being on duty, how the hell is that gonna work for me? I am a soldier not a watchman.

"Now all you need is some rest, so does Troy. I don't comprehend why you were sent here when they knew you had a bullet in your hand," Fiona's voice brought me back.

"They didn't know he had a bullet, the bandage on his hand made us all think he was fine," Troy elaborated, "As for Blade being here, Colonel wished for him to patrol here for a month because of breaking damn rules," Troy explained exasperated, I grit my teeth.

"Why? What did Blade do now?" Fiona frowned.

Troy sneered and revealed everything to her. I looked down, what had happened two hours ago, pissed me off. I am exhausted, wounded and everything that occurred around me almost suffocated the hell out of me. When Troy finished, I looked up to find they all looked at me. Fiona gaped at me for a few seconds, sighed, shook her head, and walked away.

Great, just bloody great.

I turned my head to the girl, who gathered trash and bloody dressing, preparing to leave. What should I say? How are you? No. I was in my own mental fight when she rotated and looked me straight in the eyes. I gulped.

"Thank you for everything," she glanced at Troy. "Thank you both," her eyes met mine once again. When her green eyes bore into mine, I felt my stomach tip over. What the hell?

Blade, utter something!

"It was our duty Ma'am and it's good to see you are fine," I told her, she nodded and walked away and I exhaled.

"She can talk," Troy whispered.

"No shit," I deadpanned.

"Man, why the hell were you looking at her like that?" Troy interrogated. I glared at him then leaned back on the bed.

Things are going to get riveting now.

When a man is enforced to rest on a bed and not do anything, they become very temperamental. Especially a man like me, who never desires to get tied down to the bed. Two days crawled and I have been on bed since then, I was unable to hold my rifle because of my damn injured hand.

My team had departed a few hours ago, leaving me behind for the first time in my life. Troy had bid his farewell to me and had been a little sarcastic, he attempted to cheer my mood up. I was disconsolate and devastated to an extent that even Fiona was terrified of me. The look on my face scared patients around me. Of course, I was given the best treatment that won't help my mood and fury that annihilated my forbearance.

Here I lay on the bed, and literally entreated to get up and do something useful. I couldn't because I was ordered to rest. I was also aware that when I was over with this shit, I will be off to do some patrolling. Which I should add sounds exceeding fascinating at this moment.

Tomorrow will be that day!

I rested my left arm on my forehead, closed my eyes and attempted to calm my head. My bed was far from the other patients, even after Fiona had pulled out the bullet, other doctors had come in to check the wound.

I sighed. It was then I felt a presence standing next to me.

"Fiona, I need to be alone for now, come later," I dismissed her in an vexed tone. After a while my eyes opened a little, a shadow was still there.

Stubborn as ever.

I was about to snap at her. Fiona seized my right arm, gently then started to replace the bandages. I threw my left hand that rested on my forehead and opened my eyes fully. However, they widened at the sight.

Promptly I sat straight, wiped the annoyed look off of my face, when I cam face-to-face with the owner of the green eyes. The girl blinked and looked down at my hand; she cut off the bandage around my wound and put it on the tray, her gloved hands working professionally.

"What are you doing here?" I blurted. Way to go with the question prick! She simply pointed at my arm.

"Doctor Fiona sent me to change your bandage," she spoke in a small, timid voice.

I had to hiss when she started to clean the wound, but I didn't because I peered at her like a freak. She had casually tied her hair back and left a few strands loose on the front to frame her face. She wore the same cotton t-shirt and pants I had seen her in two days ago.

The thing is she was not intimidated by me. I am well aware of the fact that women are always edge and uncomfortable around me. On the other hand, she was merely busy with her task like I wasn't even there, or maybe she was immensely good at shielding her feelings.

The girl cut a big dressing and placed it on the wound, then cut pieces of medical tape to attach the dressing with the skin on all sides. While busy that, she didn't look at me. I wanted her to look at me, why? I really don't know. Why is it a girl, a girl younger than me has this effect on me? I am a damn soldier and my feelings are supposed to be on place, intact. Then why, why is it when she is around my feelings are at all places?

At last, which was sooner than I thought, she encased a cloth strip around the injured area, and it was over like that. We did not talk; all I did was to gaze down at her.

"I will come to check on you later," she spoke not looking up, grabbed her tray and rotated to depart.

Oh no you don't.

"Thank you ma'am."

She looked over her shoulder and gave a short nod, a strand of those river-like hair fell on her face.

"Can I know who I am thanking, ma'am?" I asked with a straight face, but inside I was apprehensive if she will trust me enough to let me know her name.

"Avalina and you are Blade," was her reply and I almost smiled but stopped myself. She knew my name.

"Yes Ma'am," I nodded, with that she left. I threw myself back on the bed, well I suppose this is not that bad.

Chapter 10

I was unchained from the bed, it felt refreshing and thrilling to hold my rifle again; in my combat suit with the cap on just to shade my eyes from the furious rays of the sun. I patrolled, inspected everything, and made certain to provide refugees what they wished from me.

The weather got chillier with the days that passed. My favorite season was soon to arrive. I sauntered around the camps and kept an eye on everything. My mind went back to what occurred yesterday, I talked to Maya. They heard I was shot and she wanted to know if I was safe, or alive. She had nothing to worry about, right? Maya, man, I missed her so much. God knows when this will be over so that I could see her: even my old man.

My thought lingered on my family as I passed a tent and halted when I heard low, anxious sobs. Instantly I worked on my instincts and followed the voice and they led me around the tent that I just passed. The soldier in me kicked in so I hid my body behind the tent, stretched my neck a little, and peeked to see a boy, the kid had his small arms wrapped around a girl who seemed to be crying.

It wasn't hard for me to recognize who it was. Her small body was curled in a ball, I noticed her long black hair that fell gracefully on her shoulders. However, something was wrong, she was crying.

I couldn't help myself so I made my way to them, gradually, aware of the deep frown that appeared on my face. The little guy was one of the other refugees we had saved along with Avalina. His tiny fingers stroked her hair soothingly and she allowed him.

They spoke silently with each other in a language I could not comprehend. I guess it was the main language of Empana. I tried to catch some words but could not, except for one word "Papa", and that single word did it for me. The boy looked up at my approach but the girl was lost in her own world of desolation.

"What are you doing here?" the young man growled. I looked at him gently as I attempted to assure him I meant no harm.

"Is there any problem?" I questioned in a serene tone.

"Yeah there is, and that is you so get away from here," the boy snapped. Seriously he did piss me off but it was not him that I cared about. I silenced him with a nod and looked closely at Avalina.

I don't know what I am supposed to do in this situation, never had any experience with crying teenagers. Still, I worked on instincts once again, I crouched down in front of Avalina, disregarding the boy who glared at me. Avalina looked up at me, when she saw who it was a sob broke in her throat, and to my astonishment, Avalina cried even more. I bit the inner wall of my cheek, and wondered what the hell am I going to do now? She looked so vulnerable. I was afraid a touch of mine would hurt her. Her hiccup tugged on my heart and I held the growl that threatened to escape my throat.

"You are making her cry," the boy hissed. I raised an eyebrow at him, confused. "I was trying to make her stop for an hour," he spat and hugged Avalina again.

Well way to go, Blade.

"Ava, don't cry," begged the little man desperately. All I did was watch, I thought I could stop her but why did Avalina cry even more?

They always say girls were utterly complicated and I never believed that, but now, here, meeting Avalina they sure are. It's freaking tough to comprehend their intricate temperament. We, men, only use one hemisphere of our brain, and things are pretty clear. I don't get why God allowed women to use both of them? This makes it complicated for us to understand them.

It is more than obvious that we are enticed to women and every dude wants to understand his girl, but I don't think there is any man on the face of the earth who gets his woman completely. Can you blame me now? I don't think so.

"You need to be strong Ma'am," I grit my teeth not wanting to be so formal with her but I had to. "Stay strong for the sake of your family. I am certain they wouldn't want you to fall apart," I consoled her. A moment later I sat in front of her, in an uncomfortable position, with all the things I wore it was crazy of me to sit crossed legs on the ground.

Avalina shook her head, as more salty tears escaped those beautiful eyes. I watched focused as it ran down her cheek.

Focus Blade.

"Papa made an oath that he would never leave me! He lied, all of them did. I told them to flee but no one listened. They had to go against them and look where it got them. They killed them." Avalina blurted angrily. She wiped the tears with the back of her hands, and her lips trembled as a gentle but bitter breeze danced around us, making her hair wrap itself around her neck.

Once again, the young man talked to her in their language and I stared. This was the first time in my life, that I, Blade Devin West, could not commit anything. When it comes to battleground I was able to do something, or in any other matter, I was able to turn things around but here, with this girl all my luck and charm went to stick itself up a cow's back. It frustrated me but at the same time challenged me.

Looking at them, talking in their language, constricted my heart. The boy ran his hand on her hand to calm her. Ironically it worked, I guess he was some sort of a friend.

Reluctantly, I rose to my feet and looked down at them, "I hope you stay strong." were my wise words before I turned around and marched away from her, with a scowl on my face, and fists clenched.

The rest of my day was boring as hell. All I did was saunter around, with a rifle in hand, and kept an eye like a damn hawk. We, myself and some other soldiers, helped fix more camps around the camp as many other refugees were brought here. I was not allowed to lift heavy things because my wound was still in the process of healing. So all I did was pass stuff, lift small materials and walk half a kilometer every now and then.

I was to get only six hours of rest and that was done at night. I shared the tent with other soldiers who were assigned to patrol here as well. Some of them were assigned to night patrolling. I guess Colonel went soft on me because of my injured arm. Well, I thought the enraged bull had no heart, I was wrong.

"Blade, wake up man," called a voice and I opened my eyes to see Hassan, another soldier who had the same duty as me.

I stretched my body and rubbed my hands down my face. "What time is it?" I asked, sitting up on the cot and setting my feet on the ground. Cots were the only thing we could sleep on other than bunks beds, which were only provided back at the base, but here we had to live with cots.

"Five in the morning. Now get up man, we gotta roll. You are one of the best snipers we have but man, you can't kill your sleep," Hassan teased.

"I'm up, I'm up." I looked up at him; he gave my shoulder a pat and walked away.

Getting out of the tent I was greeted by the dark sky and dark beautiful clouds, and they brought the message of rain. Soon the clouds would cry and spread the world in their beautiful tears. I smiled and walked toward the washroom. When I was done with the necessaries, I wore my combat suit, and rifle and headed out of the tent once again and saw Hassan waiting for me.

"Where ya been dude? Ya are late," he raised an eyebrow.

"I have been doing exactly what people do when they wake up man," I chuckled. He shook his head. Hassan was one hell of an awesome man. Being in this boring atmosphere he was the one who cheered me up and hell I loved his company. Losing Mason was a huge shock and I remember him every day. His body was sent back home and they did a funeral in his honor. I wished for days that I had been there.

"So what we gotta do is keep an eye on the hill today. Ya gotta keep an eye down while I'll look around the top. These, my man, are orders from Papi," Hassan smirked. Papi was his little title for Lieutenant. Hassan was filled with humor. There were no chances of being bored with him for just about two seconds. I just met him on the second day here. He was a good man. He had to have a name for everyone, I am pretty sure he had one for me but he wasn't going to say it.

As we kept walking, I looked up. Almost two hundred tents were set on the hill. It was beautiful but when it rained the weather sucked the air from your lungs. Today, I am more than sure it's going to rain and while I am on duty I should make sure to stay alive.

Following Hassan, I stood at the hill slope.

"See ya soon, sharpshooter," he gave my shoulder another pat with a smirk and started walking up. Sharpshoot really? I guess that was my nickname.

With a deep breath, I brought my rifle closer to my chest, turned around, and got down to business. There was no chair for me to sit on, all I had was the grasses, but right now I wasn't in the mood for sitting. As though getting the hint, my stomach demanded some food. I grabbed my meal packet and took out crackers. Man, they tasted like heaven.

Once eating some of the crackers, I placed the meal packet back in my backpack and stood in attention. Every now and then my radio would crack and orders would be showered at me and my reply as always was "Roger that." Standing here for about two hours, my feet started to feel numb a little, so I paced slowly back and forth, looking at everything, even keeping an eye on the wind every time it blew making the tall grasses sway in the direction of the wind.

Something caught my attention, or should I say, someone. I narrowed my eyes and waited for the person to come near. When they were in view a smile spread on my lips. It was Avalina carrying two buckets of what seemed like water, but what is she doing coming here? Her tent is not on the hill?

I jogged towards her. Can you seriously blame me? The damn buckets had made her bent and I could see her struggling. "Ma'am let me help you," I said and slung my rifle over my shoulder. Avalina looked at me confused, and uncomfortable, " With them Ma'am," I pressed pointing at the buckets, she nodded and that was my cue. Taking the buckets from her hand, I looked at her sideways as she sighed and I smiled guess these half-filled buckets were too much for her delicate body.

"Ma'am, where should I take them?" I asked her, and she pushed a strand of her hair roughly and said.

"There is a couple at the top of the hill they needed water. I will show you the way," with that Avalina started to walk and I followed behind. It wasn't like I was running away from my duty, helping the refugees was one of my duty as well, hell I helped a mother calm her wailing child so of course, I will help her!

Walking side by side with her was amazing. There was a slight grin on my lips showing how much I was enjoying this. Time to start a conversation Blade, the top of this hill is a long way you gotta be smooth.

"How are you today Ma'am?" I interrogated referring to yesterday.

"I am fine, thank you," She simply answered in a small voice as her cheeks colored a bit and my grin turned wider.

"How is your little friend?" I tighten my grip on the buckets preventing the water to splash.

"Aden? He is fine," Avalina answered looking up at me. I stole a quick glance at her and nodded.

The spot where we were to go was nearing and I frowned not taking note of the stone in front of me, of course realizing it when I stumbled over it. Working on quick reflexes I tighten my grip on the buckets and pressed my feet harder on the ground and stood to my full height. My frown deepened. I literally stopped myself from cursing in front of Avalina. Looking up I was shocked to see a ghost of a smile playing on her lips and I gulped, something tightened in my stomach as I stared at her for a few good seconds.

"Be careful, Sir," Avalina said the smile growing a little more now. I grinned as well loving the way the wind made her hair clung to her face, and her eyes sparkled just from the small smile. What else could I wish for?

"We should get going. Wouldn't want the couple to wait for their water, now do we?" I joked, Avalina nodded and we started to walk back again with my heart beating a little faster in my chest.

"This way," Avalina guided crisscrossing the tents and at last, reaching the tent where an old couple lived. She was helping an old couple. How very thoughtful. Seeing her doing this created more respect in my heart for her. The couple passed us with a smile as I placed the buckets in front of them. Then once again, we turned around and made our way down the hill I walked beside Avalina, a little closer this time, noticing how very short she is, an easy access to place a kiss on her forehead. Damn you Blade!

"Can I ask something?" surprisingly it was her who spoke this time. I noticed her nervousness about whatever she was planning on asking. I nodded, encouragingly. She didn't ask at once but waited for a while, thinking.

"How's your hand?" for some reason I knew that that wasn't the first question she had in mind. I looked at her trying to hide the way her caring had made me feel. She stared at me back and waited for an answer.

"Yeah," I nodded again. "It's fine, much better now. Thanks for asking." I replied. She kept silent as we walked further down the hill.

"Can I ask you something else?" she spoke again making me smile. I hope she would ask me what she had thought of earlier.

"Well, you already did." I glanced at her as she looked down at the ground, shy. My reply silenced her, which was something I hadn't intended. She might have thought that I didn't want her to ask questions, if so then she was wrong.

"I am sorry. Yes please, go ahead." I apologized. I still looked at her as she looked away and stared at the fields around us. I noticed the shining sun falling on her hair making it shine like a diamond.

Turning again at me she sighed and began: "Is he gone?" she didn't need to say who it was. I already knew. It was no surprise she would still be thinking about him. My body went rigid and I clenched my fists as Lee's face flashed before my eyes, the walls of protection I had let down around her for a few seconds came up with more bricks and strength in them.

"Yeah, he's gone away. Far, far away. He can never come back." I noticed as she shivered, and I couldn't help but think of engulfing her in my arms and shielding her from this moron of a world with my shield. She is too young to see and go through this. There's lots of pain in her emerald eyes that I hate. I want to take it away from her. Take it all away. Darn it! Blade! What's happened to you? She's just another girl. Nah.. she's anything but another ordinary girl. There's something about her that attracts me to her. The air that I breathe around her, it's different.

The silence lengthened as we walked our way back to the camps.

"I...You have been helping me from the very first time, and I am very thankful for that," the sincerity in her voice echoed in my heart.

"It's my duty Ma'am," I replied slowing my pace. She nodded and bit her lip. Did she want to hear something else?

More peaceful silence as we saw a group of kids running up the hill, both Avalina and I moved to the side for them to pass. I looked over my shoulder at the little girls and boys who played without care on their faces and I liked it, that's when I heard a sigh, turning my head to the source, I scowled.

Avalina held her cotton shirt in hand, well, the torn cotton shirt, the hem of her shirt had caught with the dried wild bushes and the shirt was torn in her attempts of freeing the fiber from the bushes. It was the same shirt she wore when I saw her in the hospital.I watched as she clenched her small fists around the fiber, bit her lip and sniffed. "This was the only shirt I had," I heard her whisper, more to herself than to me.

"Avalina," I called her by her name for the first time, it just slipped from my mouth seeing her like this. She raised her head and I saw those tears in her enchanting eyes, it was unbearable and my protective instincts kicked in.

"I-I have t-to go," Avalina spoke, looking down still biting her lip. Before she could move, I spoke up.

"No. Just wait here for a minute. I will be back soon." I stopped. Her confused eyes stared at me, I gave a nod and darted towards the tent I used to rest.

I ran as fast as I could, not forgetting to pass smiles so that people won't get it wrong. Or think something is going on. I quickly opened the tent flap and rushed in, stealing a glance around to see many of my other soldier friends were resting on cots, ignoring them and trying not to make any noise I tiptoed to my cot.

I bent down, opened the zip of my knapsack and grabbed my favorite shirt. The shirt which Maya had gifted me. It was a black t-shirt with long sleeves and was perfect for why I needed it. Quickly I turned and ran out of there towards where I had left Avalina waiting for me.

While running, I huffed as the cold wind hit my skin. The clouds have spread their wings and soon were to shed tears. I kept running only to slow my pace when I caught sight of Avalina waiting for me, with her head bowed looking down at her shirt, her hair blowing dramatically with the cold wind. Standing in the field looking like an innocent angel.

I stopped in front of her and now she raised her head to look straight in my eyes. "Here take this," I said my chest heaving. Avalina glanced down, blinked then looked at me again.

"No. I can't take that," her small voice was loud and clear for me.

I shook my head. "It's getting colder here with every passing day, and we don't want you to catch a cold," I pressed. Slowly as though going over a mental fight with herself, she grabbed the shirt from my hands. And I grinned.

"Thank you, I-I have to go," She whispered, I gave her a short nod, and watched her as she walked away, well aware of my heart blossoming in my chest.

Chapter 11

That day when I was done with the patrolling which was at dusk. I had gone straight to a private who had the duty of distributing clothes to the refugees. I asked him to give me two pairs of pants and a shirt. Once I had them in my hand I went to meet Fiona.

She eyed the clothes in my hand and raised her eyebrow.

"What's this?" she inquired.

"Clothes," I replied simply. I knew she was going to start her interrogation now.

"Yeah I can see that, but who are they for?" See, I told you so.

I rolled my eyes at her and huffed a breath. "Take these and give them to Avalina," I told her.

She looked down at the clothes in her hand, then at me. "Why her?" her voice was doubtful. Women!

"Because I noticed that she needed them," I answered. She raised an eyebrow, obviously not buying it but fortunately, she took them from my hand without replying. Thank Goodness.

When I turned to go, yet another round of her questions stopped me; but this time I really didn't know the answer myself.

"Why are you doing this?" she questioned. Trust me, Fiona, I have been asking myself the same question for the past two weeks.

I faced her, making sure I had no expressions on my face. If she knew how I felt about Avalina. I could get in trouble. Wait! How did I feel about her? I really don't know!

"Fiona did I ever tell you, you ask way too many questions and I am never in the mood of answering them," was my sarcastic reply before I left the tent.

Fiona was my friend since I can remember; she was just like an older sister to me. That's why she had all the rights to question me about anything she pleases to know and I let her. Just like me, her mother passed away when her parents divorced. Fiona disagreed to see her father's face from that day on and entered military medical college to be an army doctor just like her mother was. She and Troy are not on good terms, no, not like enemies but it's best not to leave them alone under one roof, or they will tear everything apart.

Surprisingly, Fiona understands me very well but at the same time, she can't get Troy at all. It's beyond me how they quarrel so much. Troy is the most serene person I have ever known but when it comes to their quarreling, he turns into a wild pig.

On the sixth day of patrolling

Day: Tuesday

Time: 7:30 in the morning

I rubbed my hands together, as the cold wind cut my skin. My nose was already a shade of pink and my breath came out in small puffs in the air. It rained a bit last night making it even colder every time the wind decided to blow.

I was patrolling when Dimitri, one of the soldiers who patrolled here as well, came running towards me. I stopped and looked at him as he gasped for air. "Lieutenant called for you, it's for S-3." I frowned and at once followed him. When I entered the tent with Dimitri, the tent was already full. I stood in attention and stole a quick glance around. There was a man I recognized at once; he was the right hand of the President of Empana. I had seen him back at the base discussing private matters with Colonel.

Empana's government had asked for our help as their army was destroyed to a great extent and couldn't provide safety for their people. Our government had shook hands with them and taken an oath to protect their country from the evil eye.

Lieutenant informed us that there has been an attack on some people few miles away from here. The news was that some were still alive, badly injured but alive. They were in desperate need of doctors. Four soldiers were to protect the doctors in this mission. Me, Hassan, Dimitri, and Siwon.

When I was dismissed from Lieutenant Hayden I ran back towards medic tent, ordering Siwon to prepare two military Jeeps for us. When the smell of medicine hit my nose I looked for doctor Fiona, and soon spotted her, talking to an old woman. I knew she saw me that was why I made my way towards the shelves where tons of medicine supplies were piled.

"Fiona we have to move now, gather four nurses with you," I told her when she stopped behind me, grabbing the medic bags, filling them with medicine I knew we would need. My tone had told her everything that's why Fiona turned worriedly and darted away.

Soon Fiona placed two huge medical bags on my feet and again vanished. I grabbed the bags and walked out of the tent. The jeep was parked in front of the tent, I threw the bags in it. Another Jeep was parked behind mine. Dimitri and Siwon were already in their

Jeep but Hassan was helping me, checking the jeep coolant if there were enough water in it, if not then the radiator would overheat. That would cause problem for the engine. He also checked the oil gauge, not to forget the battery jumper cables.

"We are all set," a familiar voice said from behind me. I turned to look at Fiona with two other doctors and...Avalina!

"Yes Ma'am," I said. In a second, taking a note of what Avalina was wearing and it warmed my heart, seeing her wearing my shirt, even though it was too loose for her, making her look even more skinnier. I turned around and took my place behind the driver's seat well aware of Fiona climbing in the Jeep along with Avalina. These two were sitting here while the other two doctors in Dimitri's Jeep.

"Let's roll," Hassan said sitting in the passenger seat. I gave a nod and started the engine. After about five minutes we drove out of the refugee camp. My senses were wide awake, we were still safe because we were in the boundaries of the army base but once we cross the boundaries, danger can appear from any where.

Hassan had his rifle in hand while mine rested against the gear. It was 8:00 in the morning and weather was cold. The rain yesterday night still haunted the earth and the wind twisted it in a cold, sharp wind. My radio crackled and I pushed the button. "Once reaching the AO, medical back up will secure the patients and take them back to the camp," Dimitri's voice sounded from the radio.

"Roger that," I replied and kept my eyes on the deserted road.

The attack had happened in the woods, where almost thirty men, women, and children were hiding from the terrorists. They had emptied their bullets and left soon after that but lucky our base had tracked some moments from them and we were moving right away. Not many were alive but helping the few was still worth it.

It felt good to go on a mission rather than sit and patrol. The rush and excitement I used to feel on each mission was once again alive in my veins. Everything we would be doing has to be reported back to them, as we don't have a squad leader.

I drove in the woods and stole a glance in the rear view mirror; Fiona and Avalina were holding hands. My worries increased even more when I found out Avalina would be joining us on this deadly mission. But I guess she had to, whether she couldn't stay alone back at the camp without Fiona, or Fiona wanted her to learn how to take care of injured patients.

Wild woods are never safe for anyone, whether they are soldiers or normal people and especially when the world around you is literally hell. "We are getting closer," Hassan spoke from next to me and I nodded again.

After about two minutes I cut off the engine not looking towards the dead bodies. I grabbed my rifle, got out and walked behind to help the ladies. A dark cloud was looming over the sky and I prayed for the first time in my life for it to not rain and drench the earth. We need clear weather for this.

I stretched my hand out to help Fiona climb out of the Jeep. Then it was her, her face was expressionless but her eyes, deeper than ocean, they said everything , drop by drop from that ocean. How terribly terrified she was. I grabbed Avalina's hand and carefully helped her.

When I was done I stood protectively in front of them. This place was torn apart, the tents which were supposed to be sheltering the people were now drenched in their own blood, the repulsive smell of blood burned my nostrils, bodies lay around tents and only two people were there, too stunned to notice our arrival.

Fiona darted towards a man who lay flat on his back few feet away from us covered in crimson blood. To check If he was still alive, then the other two doctors rushed to help. I brought my finger on the trigger and looked around, widening my senses like a deadly viper and eyes like an eagle. Every thing around me was a disaster, the four soldiers on duty looked around and protected the doctors and a girl.

Clouds were hiding the sun , but then again the sun would push the clouds away and smile down on us. It was getting colder here, I was warm but my nose was slowly turning into ice. My gaze fell upon a doctor who was struggling with an unconscious man, trying to sit him up. I walked up to her, the doctor looked up at me. "Ma'am let me help you," I presented, bent down and cautiously sat the man and held him that way, until the doctor was done.

"Thank you," she replied when I laid the man back on the ground. I gave a short nod in answer. Then again got down to business.

Minutes ticked by in which I made sure there weren't any bodies around the tents, or anything dangerous, that was when.

"I need help here." Yelled a voice, which broke my walls of concentration and drag me towards it. My head snapped towards Avalina, she was kneeling over a man, her hands pushing the ground to support her weight, the medical kit on her left.

I darted towards her, placed my rifle next to me and squatted down. "He is breathing, the pulses are slow, I need you to help me," Avalina panted, pushing a strand of her hair behind her ear angrily. All the training I had done I knew exactly what she meant. Avalina's brows were frowned and she was concentrating on what she was going to do now. She was not shaking, she was not nervous; Avalina knew exactly what she was doing.

"We need to put him on the cot, it's too bloody and dirty here," she said putting the cap of the syringe between her lips, then tossing the cap aside.

"On three," I said, Avalina stood up grabbed the injured man's feet, then her determined eyes looked at me.

"One. Two. Three," with that I used my strength to bare the man's weight because she was delicate and fragile and as a gentleman I couldn't let her feel this patient's weight. Doing so we successfully placed the body on the cot. "Grab some cloth straps," Avalina demanded with her hands tearing the man's shirt with a scissor, revealing a big wound, this guy has been shot in the ribs, critical but she had to do it. We were short of doctors today, many had already been sent to places, so these four ladies were only the ones who could help us, which left only two army doctors back at the refugee camp.

I stood up and turned around the cot and sat in front of her, handing her the cloth straps and things she needed. I watched as Avalina started cleaning the blood, wondering how on earth she knows all this? I remember Fiona mentioning something about her father being a doctor, guess he made sure to teach his daughter some major skills.

"Hassan," I called for my partner.

"Yes," he appeared in front of us.

"Report back we need medical team as soon as possible, they have lost blood and this critical condition won't let them live for long," I ordered him.

"Roger that, boss," Hassan gave a nod and walked away to do the duty he was given.

'The bullet ,' I heard Avalina whisper again and again knowing she was afraid of going that far.

"Give me the hemostat, I have done this many times. "I wore some gloves and grabbed the hemostat and probe from her hands. "Watch and examine everything carefully you are going to need it, " I murmured, starting my job.

Soldiers get shot every day and we have experience in taking the bullet out of their body, pour some alcohol on the wound that would ease the pain a little then wrap some bandages around it. I still remember my first time, a friend of mine in my old squad was shot in the hand, my man Mason was busy with some other soldiers so I had done it instead of him.

I grabbed the bullet with the hemostat and slowly pulled it out, the man hissed in pain. I looked at Avalina, and as though under-standing me she splashed some alcohol on the wound to ease the pain. When we were done, there was a layer of bandages around his torso and the blood was cleaned a bit.

"Good job," I praised standing up and smiled down at her, she was short or should I say I was taller. Avalina nodded and turned to help yet another patient. I watched as her eyes widen and her body stiffened, following her gaze I found what it was that had shocked her. At once I ran towards a young girl, her bleeding shoulder was an evidence of bullet piercing it. I looked around for Fiona but she was busy with worse conditions. I am not doctor; I don't know what else is wrong with this kid. I clicked my lips and sat down next to her, as a layer of sweat made its way on my forehead.

I snapped my head towards Avalina, who stood ten inches away from us, looking down at the girl. Avalina was very pale now and her eyes had long gone into misery. The medical kit was in her hand; her white knuckles showed how tight her grip were around the handle.

"Avalina, I want you to help me here," I spoke in a damn serious tone. But she didn't even move nor did she blink, her distant eyes screamed the pain she was feeling, and then it hit me. The day we saved her, Avalina had witnessed the death of all her family members; in them was a body of a girl, a young girl, almost the same age as the one lying in front of me.

To hell with it, what the hell am I supposed to do now?

Chapter 12

"**A**valina, I need help here," I begged her. "Avalina, look at me," once again I tried, while my hands put pressure on the girls shoulder. Avalina did not listen to me, damn it. I knew damn well that I would regret doing this but that had to be done. I gritted my teeth and once again looked at the stunned girl, who like a ghost in front of me. "Avalina! Wake up and look at me, God damn it!" I raised my voice, which was deep and held anger and frustration in it that seem to snap her out of her misery. She looked at me as tears burned her beautiful eyes. "I-I can't do this," Avalina whispered in a shaky voice, taking a small step back. My annoyance vanished like clouds when the sun shins. Her tears swallowed me in their hurricane and yet again I was desperate. This situation is already too hard; her break down will make it hell for me. "Avalina, you are here to help this girl. If you pull back now and panic she can die, so please stay strong. Stay strong for me. I need your assistance here," I apprised. Sitting on the ground, which was a mixture of mud and blood. "I-I," She stuttered, her lip trembling and it hurt me more than the bullet that pierced my hand weeks ago. "Avalina, snap out of it," I barked roughly, feeling the blood of the little girl on my fingers. She nodded unsure then squatted next to the girl. There were tears in her eyes as they were looking down at the girl drenched in red water. With that we started nursing the girl. Halfway through the treatment, and to my relief, Fiona came and she took over, with Avalina helping her. I took out my gloves, threw them in the trash, grabbed my rifle and stood a feet or two away from them, scanning every inch of the woods with the intensity of a hawk searching for it's prey. All thoughts of Avalina vanished from my mind once I got into patrolling mood. Half an hour passed Fiona was giving her best to the little girl. At last they put the girls head on a bundle of clothes and Fiona ran to help other people.

My blood flared in my veins at the news. Apparently something more serious had happened which had caused the medical teams delay. Upon hearing the news the soldiers helped me fix the tents which thankfully were not burnt. We brought the six critical patients in the tents, while others, who had some minor injuries, were sitting around the roaring fire (which Dimitri and Siwon had put on) along with the doctors. The dead bodies were long gone, hidden in body bags, and there were only twelve people who were saved from this doomed fate. It was freezing out here with the winter day; the sun was eager to set earlier, now it was 15:00 pm. While three other soldiers and myself stood around the doctors, looking out for danger. The doctors had taken care of the water and food for the patients. Some were terrified and needed the support the ladies were giving them, taking care of them in any way possible. This shit was extremely dangerous. I sniffed and clicked my dried lips, getting annoyed with every passing second. That's when my anger got the best of me and I growled, all my fellows turned to look at me.

"This shit is insane," I spat. The three men walked towards me and stopped a feet away and were all ears. "Whaz up?" Hassan asked, frowning. "If we keep the already dying patients here, I don't think they will live. This cold is taking the best out of us." My voice was deep with anger. "But, Blade, the medical team isn't here yet," Siwon stated the already known fact. I sighed. "I know my man, but this can't keep on going," was my reply. "Then what do you suggest?" Dimitri's thick voice made me look at him. "We have two Jeeps and four soldiers, so I suggest we at least take four back to the camp. Me and Hassan will remain here, while you both drive back to the camp," I suggested. They looked at each other for a while. "That's risky," Siown pointed out. "Aren't we already putting our life in risk?" I asked, narrowing my eyes a bit, he sighed and I kept talking. "Look, we have to make a move. The orders were to stay here but we can't." "I think it's a Jim-dandy idea," Hassan agreed. "You have a point, and besides, when the team gets here I don't think anyone will have survived the cold," Dimitri agreed. "Okay, how many patients can one Jeep carry?" Siwon questioned. "Two," was Hassan's reply and I nodded. "Then let's wrap up and get moving gentlemen," I encouraged. It took us ten minutes to carefully help the patients in the Jeeps. When the four injured men were in the Jeeps they set off towards the camp. I knew they were going to be long rides, as both drivers were to drive slowly for the sake of the people in the Jeep. Now we had only one man who was resting in the tent, with other people who couldn't take the cold and had gone into the tent for warmth. It was cold, freaking cold, but my brows had beads of sweat on them from nervousness and anxiety. Any minute, any second from anywhere they can appear and kill us all-and hell, Hassan and I won't be able to hold them back. I was regretting it, regretting why the doctors were here, but they had to be, for the people who needed them. I paced back and forth looking around as the sun was fading behind the mountains to welcome yet another part of the world. The wind made the trees dance with them and the chirping of crickets welcomed the cold night. Hassan was giving the patients foods, some chocolate, crackers and jam. We had made sure they would eat something; they needed to eat and so did the doctors. They were both our responsibility. If anything were to happen to them we were in trouble. If anything happened to Avalina I don't think I'll ever be able to forgive myself... When Hassan was done taking care of the people he stood next to me. I at last stole a glance at Avalina, to see Fiona holding her hand, and saying something to her. I couldn't really hear what they were talking about and didn't want to. I watched as Avalina gave the chocolate in her hand to a woman, who was healthier and needed more to eat which left Avalina with nothing. "Man, looks like you have ants in your pants," Hassan said, not looking at me. I snorted. "Oh, hell I do," I spat bringing my rifle closer to my chest. Hassan nodded and walked around to check on other things. My attention was drawn to Fiona as she stood up and checked on the people around her, leaving Avalina completely alone and a bit far away from others. I inhaled. Slowly making my way where she sat her head bowed, and hand clasped together. I stopped on her right side, squatted down. Avalina looked up at me, her eyes narrowed a bit in a damn cute way. Not taking my eyes off of her, I took out my gloves, which were warm, then grabbed her hands. "W-what are you doing?" Avalina questioned frowning. "Just trust me, I am not going to hurt you," I told her softly and slipped the gloves onto her soft, small hands. "I know you won't hurt me," Avalina whispered. A lopsided smile made its way on my lips at her innocent comment. She didn't know how much it meant to me hearing her say that. Trust has more strength than love. It's important for a person to trust me in order to have positive feelings. "This will keep you warm." I said in a low voice, as her eyes widened. Avalina looked between her hands then at me. I sat down, then opened my backpack and grabbed the only chocolate bar I had for dinner. "Eat this," I stretched my hand to show her the chocolate. "You don't have to do this," Avalina protested in a soft voice. "Yes, I do. Here, have it," I pressed handing her the bar. She closed her fist around it, then passed me a small smile and my heart leaped.

"Thank you," "Anytime Ma'am," I replied, reading her face for a while to make sure if she was alright. I sat in front of her and crossed my legs. "When will they come back?" Avalina murmured. I knew she was asking about the soldiers. "I don't know. Hope it's sooner than we think," I admitted as I rubbed my hands together. Silence lapsed between us in which I looked around. Then, from the corner of my eyes, I found Avalina closing her hands and opening them again. "You know you did well today," I spoke, breaking the silence. Avalina looked at me confused, then sighed. "I didn't do that well, I froze" was her sad reply as a frown made its way on her beautiful face. I got what she was referring to and shook my head, looking her in those eyes which lead my world into different paths. I kept staring at her knowing. If Troy saw my face, the emotions I was displaying would give away my feelings for the girl sitting in front of me. "No. You didn't freeze. You did amazing for someone who has been through a lot recently and this happens with everyone, so you don't worry about it," I encouraged her, folding my arm over my chest to give them some warmth. "I-I couldn't help her, seeing that girl I panicked," Avalina said sadly, biting her lip and looking at the roaring fire. But I only looked at her, aware of what she was talking about. I had nothing to tell her, my words won't do justice to what she had experienced or lost so I stayed silent. Few seconds passed then I asked: "Are you okay?" A cold wind danced around us and I saw Avalina shiver then give a short nod to answer my question. We men know that when a sad or crying woman says she is okay they are not. Avalina shivered again and I mentally cursed for not bringing a jacket with me or something else to protect her from the deadly cold. "You should eat, you must be starving," I reminded her of the chocolate bar in her hand which she seem to have forgotten about. She raised her head and looked at me and my breath caught in my throat from the emotion that ran in them; her green eyes were pouring out the feelings her heart caged. And there was something else, something I was unfamiliar with. What could that be? At this moment I wished nothing else but to make her happy. I was ready to give up everything for her, anything to make her safe and I knew... hell, I knew I could even die for her. "What about you? Have you eaten?" She inquired in a small, soft voice, clicking her dry lips and I gulped. "I will manage," I replied with a small smile and stood up, trying to calm my racing heart in my chest. Holy shit Blade, you are falling for her. Rubbing my chin I walked around and stood behind Avalina. I knew she was freezing; her hands were red but she said nothing. Other doctors had brought long dusters with them, but Avalina, she had nothing. Yes, my shirt was long but it wouldn't stop her from turning into an ice. I was thinking of giving her my gloves not a few hours ago but had not seen her alone. Now I was satisfied. With a final glance at her, I started with my patrolling again.

Chapter 13

scowled deeply when my eyes fell upon my fingers. Holy shit! The tips of my fingers were pink and the rest was pale as the blood started to freeze in my veins. I exhaled, looking at my breath turn into small puffs in the cold winter air. I clicked my lips and they almost turned into ice. Ignoring it, I slung my rifle over my shoulder and rubbed my hands together.Standing far away from the fire, I once again looked around. It was Dusk and the light was fading away quickly. We had heard from the Base that the medical team was on their way but it was taking them too long for my liking. I was hungry, tired, cold freaking cold and worried to death. No, not for my death, but for the people around me. It's been a while since I feared for myself and today saw no change to that.

I have seen death many times and got lucky every time. Guess I had prayers with me or death was too busy to take me yet. I knew if today something were to happen I wouldn't hesitate for a second before throwing myself to shield the others. I was feeling the rush and excitement of this mission, even though the cold was literally making me turn into ice. I kept my distance from the patients for a specific reason. I can't bring Avalina into my thoughts when I am working so I let my man Hassan do it. He was worried but brave and very good at what he did. We both made sure to give every-one whatever the hell they demanded, even though half of which we didn't have. They were scared I could see that and now even Fiona was beginning to bite her lip with those small eyes filled with explainable fear.Seconds ticked, the tension getting heavier. That's when my sharp hearing caught a movement behind the people who sat around the burning woods. The voice of leaves crunching was loud, everyone was dead silent. I drew my rifle, eyes focused and finger on trigger. Ready to put whoever it was in a deep sleep. My steps were slow but filled with caution. Adrenaline pumped in my veins and anger started to rise.I took a quick glance at Hassan who was copying my moves but not moving from his place, which was next to the doctors. With every step I took I was getting nearer to the place where the sound came from. Stopping a feet away from the large bush in front of me, I realized something was wrong. I could feel it, feel everything; the fear radiating from the people behind me and the person hiding just behind the tree, with his back towards us. I was't sure who he was: a bastard or someone we should be protecting. So I stilled my movements, waiting for the man to make a move.Swiftly I slung my rifle over my shoulder then I raised my right hand and gestured for Hassan. Making a pistol with my fingers then resting my left palm on the back of my right hand to let him know we have an 'enemy'. Then showing him my thumb to let him know that our enemy is a male and lastly I raised my index finger and moved it in circles and cupped my hand in the air for him to know I would need his help if things got out of control. And I would need his help fast.If I pull the trigger I could attract many of those bastards here which would be welcoming my death to a tea party. Not to mention the piercing sound of fire would terrify everyone, so I had to go the other way. The close combat that I was trained specially for these reasons to do.I reached for the sheath on my right calf and pulled out my black army knife, perfect. I advanced like a lion stalking the deer, not making any sound. Every step I took was silent as though walking on clouds instead of sticky forest ground. My heart started to beat faster as I got nearer the tree. Things had to happen between seconds, more than that and I could get into trouble. He can run, or worse, turn to fire at me.My hands were not sweating because it wasn't the first time I was doing this, but I was anxious. Things could go wrong and there might be more than just a man. Standing directly behind him, with only the tree separating us, I inhaled silently, wrapped the cloak of courage and then it happened.My hands worked faster than I thought, with the knife in a 'hammer grip' in my right hand. My left hand grabbed his forehead and pushed his head in the tree, preventing him to move. But this guy was huge and he was certainly making it a whole hell of a lot harder to restrain him He panicked and grabbed my hand on his forehead, which gave me an opening. Quickly like a lighting blot I brought the blade of my black knife near his throat and slit it open. I couldn't see but I knew I was done, as warm liquid drenched my hands. I let him go and walked around the tree to see him slumped over, the blood pouring from his neck.I bent down and lowered his bandanna which was the proof for me that he was not one I should be protecting. It was their sign, a bandanna hiding their vicious faces. The man seemed in his late thirties. I stared in his eyes till they closed on their own. Looking down at my hands to see his blood on them I smirked, well at least they are warm now.Cleaning the blade with his bandanna, I made my way back to the people who waited for me and was startled to see Avalina jump to her feet and rush toward me. "Blade, you're bleeding," she gasped and I smiled. Her terrified eyes stared at me in disbelief thinking. I might have lost my brain. I shook my head."It's not my blood," was my reply as I cleaned my hands on my combat pants and my eyes narrowed at realization that she called me by my name. My stomach did a flip but it felt good. I looked up to see Hassan standing next to her and noticed how Avalina flinched."Threat down," I informed him."We have to sky out," he spat angrily."As soon as the team is here," He gave a nod and walked away. I knew he had to report this back at the Base. "Are you okay?" I asked Avalina, while she patted her enchanting eyes at me."You are the one with blood on hands and you are asking me if I am okay," she mocked and I chuckled. Yes, I did."Yes, I guess I am asking you," I replied and let my eyes look around for Fiona. Thankfully I found her quickly and saw that she was trying to stop a young boy from crying. That's when I heard a vehicle approaching and reflexively my body stood like a shield in front of Avalina. I looked at the source of the sound then I sighed in relief. The medical team had arrived at last."They are here." I looked over my shoulder down at her, Avalina nodded and turned to grab the packed stuff.

Nearly at midnight I was done with all the work they demanded. We were back at the refugee camp; patients were taken cared of, doctors were back. We had been acknowledged for our work and now I was walking with Lieutenant towards my tent to get some rest."Your performance was highly impressive today." Lieutenant Hyden made me turn to him with his unexpected comment."Thank you, sir," I answered, a bit confused which was of course visible on my face."They had been keeping an eye on you, Blade, since you started patrolling here. First we all thought you might not be as devoted to work as you are but surely you proved us all wrong and I am glad you did." Hayden kept on praising and now I got where this was going."Glad I could be of any help," I said simply."Keep that in mind, Blade. They are watching you and they are soon going to make a decision so I suggest you be careful for what you commit," Hayden warned and then strode away, leaving me with wide eyes staring at his retreating back.What was that about? With a fogged brain I threw myself on the cot, not in a mood to take off my shoes. Watching me? Like some hawk? I growled and flipped my body. Laying on my stomach I drifted in a dreamless sleep.The next morning came sooner then I thought. Weren't winter nights supposed to be longer? I thought to myself. Oh, wait, but the clock is the same. Waking up at 5:00 in the morning, I was frustrated and confused. I knew what Hayden meant by watching me; they were considering a promotion for me. I was happy but something was wrong. Maybe Troy not being promoted was bugging me. It was exactly the same reason. I hadn't seen my man from two and a half weeks now and my blood was flaring at the thought of me getting promoted without my brother.Hassan tried to throw jokes when we started with the patrolling but I was not in mood. My thoughts were running in my head, like a wild dog was chasing them. The sun smiled down at me and I scowled. I needed clouds to make my mood drift. Even though the cold was numbing my brain I didn't want the sun. Criss-crossing the tents and watching the refugees waking up and preparing their breakfast, I suddenly remembered I hadn't eaten anything from yesterday. The funny part was, though, I was't hungry at all.I walked in silence but that's when Hassan's weird laughing reached my ears, even though he was five feet away from me. I turned around and followed his gaze to which my eyes widened. First I was astonished to see Avalina in the state she was in. Second, my heart cringed for that poor piece of fabric.Avalina was kneeling, with her hair tied in a pony tail behind her head, but the wind teased her face with her strands. She was scrubbing my shirt, the shirt I had given her, on a rock with such force I thought she had intentions of literally killing the poor soul. Water splashed on her face when she beat the shirt on the rock. Here I couldn't help it and joined Hassan with the laughing. She had her brows furrowed and somehow looked extremely beautiful. What made me most proud was that she was washing my shirt.Our maniac laugh soon reached her delicate ears and her head snapped towards us. I sobered at once but my pain-in-the-butt friend couldn't stop showing his damn teeth. Avalina looked between both of us and her eyes at once filled with tears. Oh!When she looked down, resuming her beating, I punched Hassan in the arm, making him shut up for the best."Dude, what was that for?" he demanded, rubbing his arm."Laugh again and I'll kick you in the balls," I warned and walked up toward the girl who drove me insane. I stopped and looked down at her. She ignored me. I loved this, loved seeing her angry. It made me excited."C'mon, it's funny watching you beat my shirt to death," I joked, bending down so we were at eye level. She looked up and a sad pout appeared on those lips and I knew I had to do something soon."Give it to me, I'll make sure it's clean and then I'll give it back to you," I said. She disagreed with a shake of her head and I smiled."But I wanted to help, you do so much for me I wanted to wash the blood from yesterday so that I can return your shirt back to you, I thought I should at least do this for you," Avalina replied, looking at my wet shirt sadly. The smile on my face turned into a huge grin."I always wash my clothes in the washing machine so it's okay if you returned it back dirty," was what I told her."But I don't want you to wash it," she argued and something punched my heart.Then I asked with a smirk "Why?" As the word left my mouth I noticed her blush, which made her look even prettier. It made me proud."Well, you always work and get really tired; I didn't want you to..." She trailed off and after a moment of thinking she said, "I just wanted to help.""Thanks a lot for helping, Avalina." I told her, trying to hide my smile.I didn't talk but watched her wash it. The beating was actually good; the dirt was disappearing from the shirt. Every now and then she would glance up at me and smile me a beautiful, small smile which made my heart and stomach warm, regardless of the cold."So, how's you bodyguard?" She looked at me, surprised. She had no idea I noticed what happened around her. "Aden is fine and he is not my bodyguard," she replied, pouring water on the shirt. I quickly reached for the bucket and helped her with it. I guess today was the day I found out I could actually help women in their work. Maya would like to know this."But he sure seems like one," I replied, reminding her of the day I saw her with Aden. Avalina shook her head and looked up at me pausing the beating. She muttered, "No, he is just protective," and shrugged. I nodded with a smile."Don't you have work to do. I mean I don't want to stop you from your duty," Avalina added, her eyes pained a little.I sighed, she had a point but spending five minutes with her wouldn't hurt anyone. "Yeah I do, but helping the refugees is also my job,""Oh." Her brows creased . When she was done with the shirt Avalina hung the shirt on the line to dry. "Thank you." She turned to me."No problem," I told her, then watched her walk away from me, feeling the pits of my stomach fall apart. I growled when my ears heard a low whistle and knew Hassan found his new target." What was that?" He butt in when I started walking. "Nothing that concerns you," I snapped without looking at him. He chuckled."But that sure was something," he pressed and I heard the playful tone in his voice."Dude, stop acting like you have some screws loose," I grunted."That's da problem, Blade, I do have my screws loose," he laughed and I growled again. "Tell me, do ya have eyes for her?" he mocked I tightened my jaw. I am not that greedy. Sometimes Hassan really knew how to be in someone's hair.I turned to face him and the look in my eyes made him shut his mouth. "I appreciate it, I really do, but that's my personal business. Go near her or even ask me about her and I swear it won't be sunshine in your brain anymore." My threat made us stare at each other for a while, then he looked away."Chill man, don't go bananas," Hassan smiled, understanding this topic was not to be touched again. I sighed and walked again, he met my pace. "Let me tell you this, Blade, you are the only man in this world I definitely won't wanna piss off so don't worry that brain of yours, she is protected," he added. I looked at him sideways and passed a smile in gratitude.This made me worried, now Hassan knew how I felt about her. This could put me in trouble but I guess for her it's worth it. For many years I have killed the feelings in my heart but now I was more than one hundred percent sure it was the time to unleash them and face the world. Glare the animal in the eye and embrace what the feelings can do.

Chapter 14

"Stop this shit man," I barked, struggling to hold a wild, pissed off Siwon who was trying to make minced meat of a refuge e."Let go Blade. Let me teach this dipshit a lesson," Siwon hollered pushing on my hands, but I was faster and stronger."Hassan, Hassan, get that idiot out of here," I shouted over Siwon's shoulder to Hassan who was holding the refugee from coming at Siwon.This guy has totally lost the little bit part of his brain, accusing us soldiers that we have them as hostages and will eventually kill them like the bastards who destroyed their houses and families. We had found them arguing, this dumbass with another refugee. The other guy was trying to talk some sense into him but he was unbelievably blind. He had launched a grenade of curses at us when Siwon and I were passing by. Hassan was already at the scene trying to put out the fire but failed."You blood-sucking leeches," I heard him yell, a frown made it's way on my face. That second, my grip loosened around Siwon, seeing that as a chance he leaped like a Cheetah on a Deer, then delivered a nose-breaking punch in return, He got one on the face. SHIT!Before anyone from the crowd around us could scream I threw myself between them and pushed Siwon back, he was bigger and more hard to restrain. A wave of pain traveled through my jaw and shook my gums burning my face despite the freezing cold around us. This idiot has no idea where to swing his fist."Siwon! Stop, asshole! you're hitting me!" I grabbed his left hand and twisted it on purpose, he growled and threw me backward so that my body collided with the man he was fighting. So this was his aim throw me like a football towards the goal.I clenched my jaw, it burst in flames of pain, ignoring it I threw myself at Siwon yet again, anger and annoyance visible on my face, grabbed his hands, and in a swift moment pinned them behind him. "Stop it now or I swear to God I'll kick you in the ass," I ordered in my deep, angry voice. Looking at Hassan, who understood, nodded and dragged the unlucky bastard away from us.I let Siwon cool down, then slowly let go of his wrists, and came around to face him. "That was stupid," I blamed, breathing rapidly. Siwon averted his gaze and snorted in rage. I rolled my eyes at his lack of control over himself."What are you all looking at? Go do your work! " Siwon ordered the crowd around us, he exhaled and walked away.I stood there for a few minutes and was turning to go. "Soldier," called a voice and I inhaled, turning around to see Avalina standing a few feet away from me, there was a look in her eyes, a look I couldn't understand. I walked up to her clicking my jaw, which hurt pretty bad. Approaching her I saw her eyes looking at me, worried."That was insane, he hit you pretty hard, are you okay?" Concern oozed from her tone. I flinched because she'd hurt my pride, and my ego and laughed at how she thought a punch could hurt me that much." I have a name, you know," I teased, raising an eyebrow. She blushed then dropped her gaze.Looking at the light pink color burning in her soft cheeks my smile widened. My thoughts went back to the time we came back from the woods. Avalina was opening up to me, talking, smiling asking anything in which I could have helped her. "I thought you would hit that stupid man," Avalina broke the silence between us. I laughed again, suddenly I was laughing a lot."Yes, maybe it was just his lucky day today," I said tilting my head to one side. She supressed a smile. I watched as she rocked back and forth on her heels and after a moment's thought she said; "I don't know why can't they see it, you all are helping us in every way you can," she commented, angrily."Some people have greater fear than gratitude," was my reply. She stared at me for a while and I bit the walls of my cheeks. Damn, she had no idea what her gaze was doing to me.Distract yourself. I looked around for distraction and soon found one looking at the chickens who were stirring, scratching in the dirt for breakfast. At a little girl's approach, they cluck and flutter away. "How's everything with Fiona?" I once again looked at Avalina as my emotions settled down."It's going great, I learned a lot of stuff from her," she offered a smile which made the sun a little dimmer in comparison."Seems like fun," I joked, she wrinkled her nose."Sort of," and agreed then looked over her shoulder and then back at me. Her eyes were apologetic and I knew what she meant." I am sorry I have to go now, Aden is waiting for me, " her tone was reluctant. I held myself from growling. How I wished to spend time with her and when I could, either Aden or some other shit would come up."I'll see you around then, take care," were my last words then she turned and walked to where the little dumbass stood waiting for her. With a sigh, I once again started my patrolling and was going out of my mind. But I knew I couldn't let my mood, and anger come between me and my duty. Protecting the refugees came first even before my life, no matter what went wrong with my life I had to put it aside while doing what I was ordered to do.

Days were flowing like sand from hands. The rain had flooded the refugee camp, damaging them. Everyday, we soldiers would make our way in the flooded water to the tents and help the men remove the water and mud from their tents. upon seeing us, little boys and girls would come to help us. Women would light a diesel heater inside their tents to protect themselves from the cold.I had not seen Avalina since the day I got my jaw hurt. Whenever I went in the medical tent to see her, I would fail greatly. Only a glimpse of those velvet hair would pass by and she won't look at me because of the patients around her. I noticed something with my unique observing skills that Avalina was getting thinner, looked exhausted and paler every time I saw her just for seconds.Not being able to see her and talk to her devastated me. Devastation that turned into frustration and soon anger would be starting to burn in my blood. Anger on how that situation affects me. How was this possible that not seeing her affects me this much? I knew I like her but what the hell is this?Yet another week had passed. One evening, after giving the people their foods. Some of the soldiers, along with me went to help some refugees dig graves for the victims and the ones who couldn't fight their wounds. Several were dying everyday but thankfully their was no virus in the air.Returning back from the graveyard; on the other end of the camp. I was looking down having trouble breathing. We kept passing people but that's when Hassan nudged me in the elbow. I looked up at him in question, he pointed towards our right and I looked. She was standing there waiting. Hassan then left saying he had some other work to do then I walked up to her.I saw Aden standing few feet away, thankfully away from earshot, this kid really ticks me off. Avalina smiled at my approach and I couldn't take my eyes off of her, her smile opened my heart like the sunflower blossoming under the sun. "How are you?" She asked, confidently not that shy. "I am better...Now," was my true reply for her, and surprisingly she laughed and I couldn't help but stare at her, her voice rang in my ears like bells. God I was loosing my brain. "I saw you at the Medic tent the other day," Yeah right! Thank God she even noticed. "It's hectic there. I am sorry I didn't have the time to see you.." she sighed. Was she really apologizing for not meeting me? Don't know why but that felt good. "I understand," I smiled, "Duty comes first," I told her and was about to say something else when a horrific sound tore the air and the earth beneath our feet shook with such force that it felt like being hit by an earthquake, a strong one. The wave of high pressure that spread out caused shock all over my body, before I could realize what was happening. Avalina screamed, with her hands covering her ears and fell down on the ground in front of me. I quickly grabbed her wrists and rose her, she was still screaming, then looked up at Aden who was crying as well, "Aden, get her out of here." I yelled to the young terrified boy. "NOW!" was all I could manage to say to the boy and then I ran towards it, towards the yellow flash almost a kilometer away from where we stood. I could see the huge sheet of fire, my throat went dry as I kept running with everything I got. We were attacked! When I reached the place, it was just like a living hell. A big fire, like a tornado of fire was spreading over the ground burning everything in it's path. I stared at it for a few minutes that's when the cries of people for help for their mothers distracted me from the growing fire. I looked around and another wave of shock took over me by seeing everything destroyed, there was no sign of tents, nothing, only dust and fire could be seen. I looked down at the ground and felt horrible, like someone had cut my heart into pieces, looking at it, looking at the people who were killed almost instantly, their bodies were in bits, the ones who were still intact with their bodies, their finger tips caught on fire and the fire gradually spread over their entire body. It was most painful to witness that those fingers that held babies, or turned pages, they'd just burned away. Red soil and dirt was now covering me, as my eyes looked around to see the car windows shattered and burning just like the fire, engulfing everything around us. Us!I felt my body was burning, and couldn't breath well at all. I was still in shock and unable to move from my place, sweat trickling down my forehead and soaking my shirt. My eyes fells up a little baby, covered with red soil, and blood. Hot tears rushing down from his eyes, looking around with wide eyes. I marched towards him. The kid was hurt. I could see his right leg was the victim of the bomb that blasted here. I carefully grabbed the little kid in my hands, looking around for help. Then I saw the other soldiers running past me, yelling orders, ignoring the blood and flesh on their feet. I blinked my eyes twice and stepped toward the nurses and handed them the boy.That's when things were in blur, soldiers helped put out the fire, which took us till midnight, while the female soldiers helped the injured people from there towards the medical tent. Some refugees were collecting the human flesh in huge plastic body bags ignoring the dirty, heavy rain and the yells around them.I was on the scene for the night and the next day. There were a lot of things needed to be done. There was no time for me to get some rest and I didn't complain at all. I was glad they didn't let me rest because laying on that small cot and thinking about what happened yesterday, about my team, maybe they are dead and here I am living. Alive, not there fighting avenging them. I had no intention of sleeping and clearing my head because I knew once I wake up it'll be worse. So this was what I needed I worked all day and would loved to keep going on the next day 'second day of my fifth week' but Lieutenant had ordered me to get some sleep. I didn't go to sleep right away because there were some patients who were brought here and their chances to live were critical. The doctors didn't even have time to breath, it got worse with time, everywhere I looked in the medical tent it was flooded with blood. Fiona and Avalina were running around for hours, helping them and trying to save their lives. I leaned back on the couch in the tent where I usually rest. I had only three hours to rest. I looked up staring in the space and lost in thoughts. I should have a chat with Maya, she would like that and I might be able to think about something else other than mourning. I sighed. The flap of the tent opened, I looked towards it to see Avalina standing there. I was well aware of my eyes going wide with shock. What was she doing here? Has something happened again? And was about to stand up when she walked in with small steps clearly nervous. My heart trashed in my chest. She looked at me innocently and stopped where I sat glued to the couch. I saw dark circles around her red and puffy eyes, her clothes had blood on them, her hands were dirty and dry. The river-like hair were tied in a messy ponytail and I knew how freaking tired she was. Avalina sat next to me, wearing the shirt I had given her days ago. We sat like that for a while loving the warm tent and the silence here. Then she took off her shoes, her feet were swollen and the toes were bloody. She turned her body to the left so that she was facing me and I turned my head right to look back at her that's when I saw her teeth clattering. "Avalina you are freezing," I said almost giving away the pain in my voice, it killed me seeing her like this. Quickly I grabbed the blanket on my right and handed it to her. "I heard you were unhappy," she murmured. I almost smiled at her voice, so soft. We both knew we didn't want to talk about what had happened yesterday the memories are still haunting us."And why am I unhappy?" I asked in a low voice looking in her bewitching eyes."I heard Fiona say you don't like to patrol here in the refugee camp," Avalina explained, disappointment in her eyes and she was getting tired every minute."Fiona is right. I came here to fight them not to patrol, it's been four weeks. I am here because of the wound I had and my punishment and will be here till the team comes back," I told her looking past her now. She simply hummed in reply..But," I began once again meeting her green eyes. "There is a special reason I like it here, believe it or not I actually wait for the sun to peek over the mountains," and added with a smile."Really? What's that special reason?" Avalina questioned, turning a bit more so that she was sitting on the edge of the couch."You really want to know?" I teased smirking. "Yeah I do," she nodded her head continuously."I think you already know Avalina," I hinted enjoying where this was going."I do?" She frowned still not getting it that it was her, only her I had managed to like this duty. It was her, the innocent Avalina who gave me peace in war time. Everyday just by having her around blossomed foreign feelings in my heart.I laughed. "Can I ask you something?""Ask away," now she was curious."How old are you, Avalina? She smiled."Three months ago I turned nineteen. What about you?" her eyes watched me."Aaa recently I just turned twenty seven," her smile turned into a grin."Now tell me what makes it special for you?" She reminded me of the topic I tried to change a minute ago. Guess it's time to let her know how I feel just a little bit."You know, Avalina," I said looking deep in her eyes. Understanding drawn to her. Her eyes widen a blush creeped onto her face. She dropped her gaze and I chuckled resting my head on the couch.The blush on her cheeks gave her an innocent look that tugged at a protective instinct deep inside me.A few seconds passed and I still had the smile on my lips when she was not looking at me. "What about your family?" Avalina asked trying to change the atmosphere."They are fine. I have a sister named Maya. She is a year older than you," I replied."Do you miss them?" She shot another question in a whisper. I barely heard it."Yeah, especially Maya," I kept going on then at once realizing Avalina had tears in her eyes. Holy shit. I hurt her without having any darn idea about it.I sat straight, turned so that now I was facing her as well. "Avalina please don't cry, anything but your tears, please don't kill me, every tear you shed each time I'll die," my begging voice was deep and soft. I grabbed her tiny and delicate hands in mine."The little girl they killed she was my niece. They killed papa, mama and Anie. I told them to run but Papa disagreed he wanted to hold them off but they shot him in front of me, they killed them all. I remember their yells, the agony which pleaded from their eyes yet those monsters laughed, laughed while killing my little niece," sobs racked her body."Avalina you saw what we did, they are dead, we took your revenge," I consoled her or at least tried. She gave a short nod and opened her eyes."I don't know what happened to their bodies," she sniffed looking at me like she was lost, desperate, her lips trembling."We couldn't do anything, it was dangerous to stay there more than ten minutes. I am so sorry," I apologized. Her eyes reminded me of the day I had seen her the first time, scared."It's not your fault. I-I just miss them a lot," her voice quivered, slowly as though unconsciously she rested her head on my shoulder and

I froze. Her being so near felt right, felt perfect. I was frozen in my place as she shed more salty tears. I couldn't dare rest my hand on her shoulder. Sure I wanted to, but man I couldn't. After few minutes I noticed her breathing became slow so I turned to look at Avalina she was sleeping on my shoulder, her eyes closed, lips parted slightly. I have been dreaming about her since I was twenty, everyday wished to meet her, the one I would fall for and here she was, so close to me.She squirmed hugging my arm and a strand of her hair fell on face disturbing my view. Reaching up I removed it from her face with the tips of my two fingers and on purpose let them linger quietly on her creamy skin. Minutes passed in peaceful silence then I closed my eyes and dozed off.........

All my life I never had a sleep like this, even though I was sleeping on the couch with my back aching a little. I opened my eyes, grunted blinking few times then felt something on my right thigh. Rubbing my eyes I looked down a smile, a true smile spread on my lips. Avalina's head was resting on my thigh, fast asleep. She looked truly beautiful with her eyes closed and lips in a pout, so innocent that it hurt my heart. Will I ever have her? Does she share the same feelings I do? Or it's just because I am protecting her?The flap of the tent opened and I tensed, clenching my fist thinking about an excuse. But to my surprise it was Fiona who walked in then stopped in her track looking at us with shock in her eyes. Oh shit. Two seasons I didn't want her to know about Avalina. First, this might get me in trouble with Colonel. Second Fiona is a little protective of her so this might not be a good thing.It was a relief to see her crack a smile. I relaxed putting my finger on my lips. Fiona nodded the slowly walked where we were, mouthing a girly "aww" Damn girls!"Blade, Oh my God!," she whispered her eyes twinkling. I rolled my eyes and shook my head in 'No'"You like her?" Fiona inquired near my ear. I didn't reply for few seconds then smiled. Trust me denying it was hard and wrong so I flashed her a smile that explained everything. She literally clapped her hands in excitement. Both Fiona and I looked at the girl. The doctor was shocked I knew that then again Fiona was a sister to me and I knew she would want me to be happy no matter what.Minutes later Fiona tapped her watch, reminding me I had to patrol again. I gave a nod with the last smile and a sisterly pat on my shoulder she left the tent. I once again caressed Avalina's cheek with my thumb. Where will this end up? What do we name our relation? Will she accept me? I sighed through my nose as anxiety throbbed in my heart and decided it's time to come out of fantasy and jump in the horrifying reality."Avalina, wake up," I gently shook her shoulder. A sleepy moan escaped her lips as her eyes opened, almost five seconds passed she sat bolt straight, looking at me ashamed. Avalina flattered her eyelashes looking at my thigh then back at me."I-I," and shuttered turning red. I couldn't help but laugh at her unique expression."You fell asleep, I didn't want to wake you up so I slept as well," I informed her, pushing myself off of the couch, grabbed her hands and stood her up. Avalina still didn't meet my gaze."I am sorry," she murmured an apology. I smiled, which I do a lot around her."Don't say that, man, I didn't have a rest like that in days," I replied, grabbing my rifle and slung it over my shoulder. Then taking hold of my pistol I stuck it in the waistband of my combat pant."Why? you don't sleep?" She demanded concerned."I do get rest but not as peaceful like the one I had few minutes ago," I told her wearing my cap. She nodded thinking about something. Probably thinking how to help me but she doesn't know she already has."Come here," I ordered. She took a small, shy step towards me and my heart raced. Avalina was doing it on her own no one was pushing her!I was tall so she reached my chest. I placed a soft kiss on her forehead leaving my lips there for a while, aware of her tense body and my dry throat. This was my first step towards our relationship, she has opened a door of her fragile heart for me a little all I have to do is to enter and make her heart mine like she has mine in her hands.Pulling away I looked down in her eyes then whispered," Take care," with that left the tent well aware of her flushed cheeks.

Chapter 15

Three days since the bomb blasted, things were a little calm around the camp, mainly because many have seen worse than what happened here.

When it came to Hassan, you can't possibly talk in simple terms with the guy in its low speed. It was the first time that Hassan and Dimitri had the same rest hours as I did so we decided to have a little gentlemen talk.

"No, I swear man, Papi is noosed," Hassan bragged spreading on his cot next to mine, while Dimitri rested on the floor.

"Yeah you are right. Not all his thrusters are firing," Dimitri stated. I looked at him for a second then burst into laughing. The title 'Papi' was popular among us soldiers for Lieutenant Hayden but Dimitri never used or made fun of him, saying that Hayden wasn't thinking clearly. That was something new for me! We couldn't stop laughing for about two minutes.

"What did he use to say when we were training back home?" I questioned propping on my elbow. Hassan snorted and started mimicking Hayden.

"Pop that target right there ladies any desmandos won't be allowed," I chuckled then shook my head when Hassan showed his 'finger' as though Lieutenant was in front of him.

"Don't forget what Hayden use to bark about when there wouldn't be any team work. 'Ladies, Ladies pull leather I want you to pull leathers.' Sometimes I wondered if he was only talking to the female soldiers or he just ignored us," Dimitri joked looking at us then again we started laughing at how Hayden would demand for team support calling it 'pull leather'.

"I swear with him shields are up but no one is on the bridge," was my reply in between my laughs.

Suddenly Dimitri stood up and so did Hassan but I was still laughing. I looked up at them questioningly. Dimitri didn't meet my gaze but murmured. "Check you six," as words left his mouth I turned around then jumped from my cot, saluted and stood in line with the other two.

Lieutenant Hayden stood there with an annoyed look on his face, hand behind his back and looking us straight in the eye.

"Spunk," he spoke taking a step forward and I held my head a little high. He thought we were brave to pick on him perhaps foolish! "Weren't you cowboys ordered to get some rest?" he stated more than questioned.

"Yes sir," was our unison reply.

"Three hours, Am I clear?" Lieutenant asked smugly.

"Yes sir," but my head snapped towards Hassan when he replied, "read you 5 by 5 sir," it wasn't disrespectful but it sure ticked him off. I bit my lip from laughing. Lieutenant glared at him then left when tent flap was down that's when we went wild with laughter.

"Dude you are crazy," I said lying on the cot after five minutes. Hassan sighed and threw himself on the couch behind my cot.

"It ain't like we are in jam by making fun of that meat Popsicle," Hassan barked with laughter. Dimitri shook his head laughing. "I'll better get some rest," he then said with a smile on his lips. With a wave Dimitri walked toward his cot.

"Let's catch some Z's man, before I pass out, see you later man," I told Hassan, resting my hands behind my head.

"Peace out," Hassan said in a murmur then we dozed off.

Tick Tick Tick.

I heard my watch tick as I rested my arm on my forehead and lay there, listening to it quietly. After finishing my patrolling which was the only thing I had as a duty, I came back in the tent which was my home and threw myself on the couch and propped my rifle against the couch. I looked up at the roof of the tent and thinking about what my man Troy was doing?

The team wasn't back yet; it has already been more than five weeks. Colonel had called me the other day back at the Base informing the team was fine and it was something that lifted a great deal of worry off my shoulders. So I did my best at patrolling but standing on your feet for hours was not what I came here to do. The reason I kept on going was Avalina, by now I couldn't spend a day without seeing her and I already knew I was falling hard for her. Like some people say 'I might be in love.'

Just when I realized I can't spend a day without her, it pained me further knowing what I was doing, what I was doing to her in particular. As a soldier I can't predict anything about my life, how long will I be breathing? My life and the lives of the people I know can change in a matter of seconds. Just one bullet at the right place and I will become a memory in the minds of those who cared for me.

Sadly, I have just come to recognize that with little encouragement, I could make Avalina be one of them too. I can't go on with what was going on between us. I have a duty to do and will have to leave once orders were given to me, I won't look back. If anything were to happen to me she will shatter because of me and I can't be the reason for it.

I have decided to keep my distance from her even though it means I have to cut a piece of my heart.

Feeling a shadow standing over me I opened my eyes, someone was looking down at me with eyes like an open field and hair like the most breathtaking waterfall, cascading down her shoulders tickling her cheeks on their way down. The light smile on her lips that made me proud. The look in her eyes which poured her feelings straight from her heart.

I sat up and crossed my legs on the couch. Avalina sat in front of me crossing her legs as well so that we were facing each other, sitting on the couch. I noticed she had a plastic plate in her hand which was filled with food.

"Are you going to have lunch here?" I asked her. Avalina came here often. Hassan would smile and leave us alone even my other fellows didn't complain in fact they knew how deeply my heart was insane about this girl.

She shook her head and grinned, her eyes lighting up. "I heard you didn't eat anything from a day," Avalina replied grabbing a plastic fork and giving it in my hand.

"No, it's okay I am not hungry and besides this is your lunch," I told her not tightening my grip on the fork. She rolled her eyes making my stomach flatter.

"I am not the one who is starving from a day and half now, and I'll be eating with you, so eat up," Avalina ordered pursing her lips, I chuckled then ate from what she brought. Damn! Whatever that was, whoever cooked that was an awesome person. I slowly nodded in reply that it was tasty. Avalina smiled and though proud and stuffed her food in her mouth, chewing slowly.

"I am going to eat all this if I don't stop now," I mumbled shaking my head in amazement.

"No problem I'll make more for you," she smiled at how my eyes widen.

"You made this?"

She nodded, "Mama taught me how to, she always said a girl should know how to cook," I watched as her brows ceased but then she looked up and smiled brightly, "Blade I can have more later, eat this and I am not taking no for an answer," was her calm reply but it held authority. I smirked then started eating while she watched me. I stared back trying my best not to show how broken I was inside. For some reason I knew that it was too late, for her and for me to pull back now. She was sitting so near and smiling at me, I had already encouraged her too much. For her sake I have to stay away but....it's hard.

"Any word from your team?" Avalina questioned, as I ate silently. She poured me a glass of water from the cooler box next to us. I growled shaking my head. She knew how desperate I was to get out of here.

"I don't have any idea when they'll be back," I said eating the last bit in the plate and I still wasn't full. Can you blame me, I am a grown up man who eats twice the size of her so this won't be enough for me! "How's the Medical tent going on with you," I interrogated, putting the plate on the cooler box next to the couch.

"Fiona is teaching me how to stitch deep wounds," Avalina said in a small voice, a smile playing on her lips.

"That's good to know," I took off my cap then noticed her staring at my hair. I was about to make a joke that's when I heard that voice.

"What's good here?" a damn familiar voice demanded. I looked up to see Troy standing on the door of the tent. I laughed and stood up.

"You're alive man," grinning I hugged him, and then patted his back twice.

"You seem disappointed?" he joked. I rolled my eyes. "We just came back half an hour ago. I came here to see if you were still breathing," Troy kept going on. I noticed he was tired, there were dark circles around his eyes and man has he lost some weight. He was oblivious of Avalina's presence but I wasn't. Her presence was mighty. I could even sense her confused gaze on us. Turning around at her still smiling, she tugged a bang of her hair behind her ear when Troy's eyes fell on her. I remembered they weren't officially introduced.

"Troy this is Avalina, I am sure you know her. Avalina this is Troy, my brother, my buddy," I introduced in a happy tone. Troy raised an eyebrow at me. He didn't know about me having feelings for her, spending all my free time with Avalina, even my dreams.

"It's a pleasure to have finally met you," Troy stretched his hand for her to shake. Avalina hesitated but then shook his hand however retreated it fast. From the looks of it, Troy understood she wasn't comfortable with men. I sat back on my place while Troy sat on the ground in front of us, with his legs crossed, he didn't have his rifle, nor his cap simply in his army suit.

"How were days here?" Troy inquested.

"Patrol and sleep, nothing else," I sighed well aware of Avalina looking anywhere but Troy. I turned my head right so that I was staring at her. When I finally looked back at my man, who was looking at me with a smirk, Oh shit! My feelings were like an open book, for someone like Troy who knows every vein that crosses another in my body, it wasn't hard to read me.

"Dude," he mouthed, I just shrugged. "So what did you do in your leisure time?" Troy inquired, I glared at him knowing where he was going.

"I didn't have any leisure time," I informed, sarcastically.

"Holy s...." I widened my eyes at him as he was about to curse in front of Avalina.

"I will be back, I have some work back at the medic tent," Avalina whispered and grabbed the plate leaving the tent. I didn't stop her knowing she wasn't relaxed around him yet.

Once she was gone; "Really?" Troy started to put me through the wringer. I inhaled then shook my head in denial.

"C'mon man you can't hide it from me." his rambling started.

"Stop bullshitting," his gaze was fixed at me, with a smug smirk he waited. I stared at him for a while then gave in, "guess from the very first time I had feelings for her, they luxuriated every time I was around her," I replied leaning back on the couch.

"Damn! Our Blade is whipped." Troy chuckled. I shook my head.

"No I am not. I am befuddled about her feelings man," I ran my hands down my face. Troy whistled then raised an eyebrow, ruffling his hair.

"Man, my Blade is in love,"

"What?" I gaped at him.

"Are you really serious about her?" Troy stated leaning on his hand and spreading his feet in front of him.

"I don't know." I sighed. "I am worried, it's not easy to like anyone. What if she doesn't share the same feelings? And you know I can't just lead her in this" I asked my best friend the truth.

"Man, a teenage girl is not crazy to spend time with a grownup soldier, of course there are feelings in her heart that's why she was sharing her meal with you!" Troy explained like he knew everything.

"Wait, how did you know about the meal?"

"Common sense Blade, there were two forks, one facing you the other was facing her," Troy kept on explaining with a smirk.

"You make sure to study what is around you, don't you?" I teased.

"That's why I am called a soldier," he replied pulling on his collar.

There was a moment silence. "I am happy for you, you never had a serious relationship and have not been in one since you joined the army, this my friend seems like a good thing and am sure it'll make you happy," Troy commented looking at the ceiling. I just wished he was right I have been waiting for the right person since I was twenty , it's been six year I haven't involved myself with girls well not emotionally. Being twenty seven I think it's time to settle down with the girl I like.

"Hope so," I murmured.

My team was moving in a day. Colonel had called for me saying how well I had done this past month and a week, and once again

I could go with my team. Hearing the news made me extremely happy. I was there at the Base even when they started talking about the explosion last week, the fact was obvious it was 'their' doing. Our best Commandos were sent to search them out and make sure to pierce every single bone in their body with bullets.

Turns out they are planning to attack ones again and this time they even dared to target the military Base. That's the main reason Colonel James was literally pulling his hair, even though he was a bald man. This shit was dangerous we were killing a great number of them. Now that ours and Empana's trained soldiers were together it seemed like we had the upper hand.

Troy, who had come with me to the Base because Zach our team leader had called for him. He was laughing at me while I couldn't stop smiling. Then the realization hit me like a lightning bolt that I won't be able to see Avalina for God knows how many days, there I can't even guarantee a shit about my life! The smile was soon replaced by a frown. Then again this was good, wasn't it? I was keeping my distance from her so she wouldn't be hurt. For her happiness, I have to kill my heart. I stayed back at the base because I still had to meet my team members and our leader Zach.

So I did, like I had agreed embracing what fate had planned for me. Zach was hurt, no, I wasn't glad he was hurt that was the reason our squad stayed behind until he was well enough to move and Zach also asked for another man in our team so things were being discussed between the higher ranks.

A day passed I didn't go where she was, buried my feelings deep inside that heart like none of this ever happened. Still, fate had something different planned, there were times when I would walk around the tents to do what I was asked and there she was, I would hide, and wait till she walked away, seeing her standing there, I knew my feelings were never going to be same, I had to move away. I was a fool thinking this would be easy on me. Can a body live without its heart? The moon without the sun. The pain was torturous. I knew it was too late to go back.

Throwing myself in front of any work or any opportunity I tried to stay away and was doing well in it, like I said fate had different plans. I had to drop some supplies at the medical tent. Pushing the feeling with a rock inside me, I grabbed them and walked in, it had been one and a half day now, not seeing her. Without looking up, and ignoring the place I knew she always worked. I quickly placed the supplies then looked up, she wasn't around me, looking around it wasn't hard to find her.

There Avalina stood, helping Fiona with their job. The feeling took over me once again, so close to going insane. I knew I was going to sacrifice my heart and let her breathe again. Whatever between us had to fade away...I was staring for God knew how many minutes, until she raised her head and was about to look my way when I turned my head and walked out of there like I didn't know she was there. It hurt.

Just like the old time, I spent my time with Troy and Hassan who seemed to enjoy Troy's company. Trying to forget that Avalina, she was a girl I saved from those monsters, that's it. Troy sensed something but never spoke it out loud. I was thankful. Troy being the man who knew so much was a pain from time to time.

The feeling was worse than anything I ever experienced. It was like every second your body was being pierced with bullets but no blood flowed, no physical pain screamed just the brain which went numb every minute.

Three days dragged, every hour like a year. Tomorrow we were at last moving, leaving this place for the best. Dusk approached like an invited guest, engulfing the sky making it smile and shine with hundreds of diamonds. I turned and walked back to my tent to get my bag pack but stopped abruptly at the sight in front of me.

Walking up the hill were none other than Avalina and Troy. What shocked me the most was Avalina, she wasn't smiling but laughing, which she never did around me, not that openly. Something like a huge rock dropped in my stomach. I clenched my fist. Rooted on my place and fuming in anger all I wanted to do right now was show stars to Troy. The thought clinged in my brain, I scowled never in my life I think to hit my man, so why now?

That's it, I can't do it. Can't do it anymore. With a growl I strode where they were, Troy smiled then it disappeared when he saw the look on my face. Whereas Avalina was ignorant of it.

"Hel-" began Avalina. I cut her off resulted her eyes go wide in shock of course confusing her first I vanish for days and now I am acting like a moron but she didn't know.

"What are you doing here?" my voice was deep with anger and something else as I glared at Troy.

"Getting to know each other better," Troy defended. I shot him a glare he stood to his full height, straightening his spine returning my glare.

"Blade where were you, I have been looking for you? What is wrong? "Avalina questioned in a low voice clearly scared and confused at the same time. I growled in frustration.

"To know each other better, Troy?" I spat pointing my finger at both of them. He shook his head as though at my stupidity.

"Blade calm the..f...," I knew he was going to curse but held it back as Avalina looked between us like a ping pong match.

I looked daggers at him; "Why don't you take an airlock walk," I clenched my jaw as he raised an eyebrow, threw his right hand in the air, and walked away from us.

Talking a deep breath I turned to look at her and found Avalina glaring at me, actually glaring at me and yeah I loved it, wanted to smile but was a little too annoyed to do it.

"What was that?" she demanded crossing her arms.

"I should be asking you, Avalina," she rolled her eyes.

"Blade we were just getting to know each other, he is your friend he thought I might as well find a friend in him. Why so angry about such a thing? I haven't seen you in days and when I do, here you are acting so different." her brows ceased as annoyance filled those enchanting eyes. I huffed.

"God Avalina why don't you get it!" I bellowed, clenching my fist hard when she flinched from me! "I don't want you with anyone, I don't want you around anyone." my lungs dried when tears rushed in her eyes. I licked my dry lips as desperation launched at me, at the lack of control over my emotions. Then without saying another word or being able to look at those eyes who had accusation in them, I walked away. I had no idea why was I that mad. Troy wouldn't do that!

Walking back in the tent Troy was waiting for me, "What the hell was that?" he was literally yelling.

"Shouldn't I be the one asking you both that same question?" I said angrily, knowing I was not making any sense.

Troy sighed, ruffling his small hair, "Blade man you know, you know I wouldn't even dream of looking at her that way. You idiot, she is like my sister!" he clarified standing up now. I averted my gaze from him.

"Don't mess with me, Troy. I know what I saw."

"You are crazy, man, listen to yourself!" he hollered pointing at me. I didn't say anything, just stood there taking deep breaths. He was right, I knew it but will someone just tell my heart the same shit.

My shoulders sagged after a while "This..Feeling like someone lit a fire inside me, I don't get it," I came clean rubbing my neck. Troy snickered coming to pat my shoulder, forgetting the fight we had just a few seconds ago.

"That my bro is called being jealous and you get jealous when you are in love," he smirked.

"Oh! piss off!" I pushed him.

"Now I am sure you pissed her off, what are you going to do?" I remembered the tears that were caused because of me being a classic idiot.

"Make it up to her I guess, talk to her now, tomorrow at dawn we are ordered to move," I told him, he nodded.

"I'll rest here tonight, we'll leave together for the Base," Troy said throwing himself on the couch. Minutes passed and now I was kicking myself mentally. Troy had fallen asleep and I sat up on my cot head in my hands and regretting every shit I did fifteen minutes ago.

Standing, I slowly walked out of the tent, thinking how am I going to apologize to her? Looking around the medical tent, she wasn't there. I even asked Aden if he has seen where she was, but the little moron just glared at me, letting me know he wasn't going to say anything. Anger on Troy and now this hit my brain like someone was punching me.

Turning around the corner of her tent, there she was looking up at the moon which smiled down at her. I stood there watching her, almost sure she wasn't real. Choosing the right moment a cold, but gentle wind danced around her, making that silky hair join with the wind. Avalina pushed the strand that teased her cheek behind her ear, and whipped her eyes. She was crying!

Slowly making my way up to her, I stood beside Avalina in an awkward silence my leg continued to bounce with agitation while she didn't even glance my way. I tried to calm my frustration but was failing big time, her smile flashed in my brain it ticked me off. Clearing my throat I turned my head right. "Are you still mad?" no reply she just looked down, at the tent few feet away from us, it was dark but I could see her, tears drying on her cheek. She was wearing a brown duster now which protected her from the dark winter.

"Avalina, I'm-I'm sorry," there was this dry lump in my throat it was the first time in life ever said sorry to a female other than Maya and I wasn't truly apologizing to her just need to say it. Swiftly Avalina turned her head and looked me straight in the eye.

"Do you even mean that?" her voice shook but I could sense anger as well. Working on instinct I stepped closer to her, we both stood face to face.

"Avalina," few seconds ticked "I am really sorry, man I don't know I-I just flipped," I told her the truth in a whisper because their wasn't must space between us, looking down in those eyes I only wished I could get lost.

"Blade, how could you think that way? He is your friend," she accused not taking those eyes away from mine. I sighed reaching to touch the fallen hair on her face, astonishingly she leaned closer at my touch, dropping her gaze.

"Avalina," I paused, "I am a very possessive man," I uttered, feeling ashamed at this confession. As those words left my mouth, the green orbs met my blue ones and an adorable look appeared in them. Avalina bit her lip and colored.

"So," I began with a slow drawl when she didn't reply. "Am I forgiven?" I asked. It took her a minute to look up and then she nodded.

Taking another huge step of my life, I placed my palm on her cheek, it was cold and so soft that silk didn't do justice in comparison. Avalina closed her eyes as I caressed her cheek with my thumb.

Heart beats fast, my left hand that hung on my side shining with sweat. I had to tell her, break the damn news to her. I'll cherish this moment until my last breath. The angel in front of me will always be in my heart, even if it stopped beating it will belong to her.

"Ava," I began. Her eyes opened and she frowned by the torn look on my face. "I have to tell you something," she gulped, giving a short nod.

"My team is back, and umm" I trailed off, "I. have. to. go tomorrow." Her eyes widened, showing the effect the news had made.

"You're leaving!" her lip trembled. I watched as she blinked her eyes few times before tears rushed in, soaking her eyelashes. I growled.

"I will be back. I promise," a silent sob escaped her lips, killing me right there.

"Ava, Ava please don't cry, I will be back," they were just words, I didn't know if I will ever see her again.

"I will have no one," she panicked, I grabbed her shoulders.

"No, Fiona, Aden they are here for you, please don't make it harder than it already is," I begged. She just nodded, not meeting my eyes.

"When are you going to come back?" her innocent question reminded me of what I decided but I slipped, being around her and not caring for her was the hardest thing I had ever done.

"I don't know," I murmured, brushing my fingers on her soft cheeks, whipping the flowing tears. None of us said another word for a long, long time. We stood there, lost in thought but not moving away. In the end I knew I had to for her own sake.

Taking a deep breath and her scent, I placed a kiss on her forehead noticing her stiff shoulder, "Ava, just like your name you are my life. Please take care of yourself," feeling the soft skin on my lips for few more seconds. I pulled back and darted away. It was too much, too hard.

Chapter 16

"Bruce, cover us. Blade turn around the house and meet us back in," Sgt Zach ordered, reloading his assault rifle.

"Copy that sir," both Bruce and I replied. Zach was now a Sergeant but still an idiot, and he was best at what he did and that kept me from punching him in the nose for his bloody attitude.

Bruce and I made our way to the back; he stayed behind as a lookout while I kept walking until I was standing in front of the back door. Before I could sneak in, a bullet wheezed over my head and hit the door in front of me, an inch away from my shadow on the wood.

"Shit," I cursed kicking the door with strength. It burst open and I threw myself in the cold house. Leaning on the wall I peeked from the door frame. Bingo! The moron was running straight for the house, giving me a clear shot. Instantly I grabbed my pistol, bringing it up, eyes narrowed in frustration that this prick almost killed me.

When the barrel of my pistol came in view from the door frame, he raised his rifle; another bullet passed me just inches away. Getting tired of this. I pulled the damn trigger, not paying much attention then gave him a clear headshot! Mounting my pistol back in the sheath, I turned around a gasp left my mouth. The place stunk like hell, blood was everywhere, and even though it was afternoon the house was dark and screamed of danger.

With great caution I took my every step, my ears picked up the sound of a woman yelling and at once I knew where our target was. Passing the stairs which were broken and spiders were busy making their webs on the corners. The wooden floor I was walking on was coated with dust so deep that I could literally dig my index finger in it. Curtains stained with blood were drawn over the windows shielding the house from the sun.

Listening carefully nothing but the yells the difference was now that someone was laughing. I gripped my rifle tighter and kept walking to see my team was already waiting by the door. Hassan was standing right behind Zach with his AK47 in hands. Passing me a smirk

Apparently Hassan was chosen as the sixth member for our team. I liked that a lot. He was a great time pass when we had nothing but to wait for being attacked. Zach raised his gloved hand and showed me his pinky. Meaning our team is supposed to save the woman behind this door. He started the countdown.

1....Now I realized how fast my pulse was running, the sweat that trickled down my forehead, freezing my already cold skin.

2....His other finger was raised. I clenched my jaw thinking of what was happening to the women and trust me. It felt like the flames of hell were burning inside me, tormenting every cell in my brain.

3....He raised his third finger; I gulped the saliva in my throat as Zach kicked the door just like Death marching and entered the room, yelling for everyone to stop moving.

Everything happened so fast, it was blur. One second we were waiting outside the other we were in, surrounding the two men who were raping the owner of this house in front of two young boys. Every one stood frozen, only Zach moved, kicking their weapons away from reach, and then delivering a sold kick or two in their face.

My man Mason would have been the one to aid the woman, guess in my absence they decided it would be Carlos. He grabbed the sheet from the dirty floor, quickly wrapping it around the unconscious lady, and then gently brought her knees to her chest, curling her in a ball

I averted my gaze, looked at the two men kneeling before Zach, they didn't have their bandannas on face, giving me a view of what they look like. Both seemed to be in their mid thirties. Nothing else mattered this minute, no one else was in this room, expect from me and them. I could feel my hands shaking from anger, teeth clenched so hard that if any longer I would be toothless.

Carlos went up to the young boys, who were wounded, badly injured. They cringed away from him but the man had a fatherly look on his face as he grabbed their hands taking them away from here, knowing soon the floor of this room would be a rainbow of blood. Troy was standing by the window looking for any sort of danger, while Hassan stood by my side, the same feelings rushing through him. I could tell because of his tense shoulders.

Zach glared down at them, his rifle targeting their brains. Then he withdrew and called." Blade," I was shocked as to why he had called me.

Taking a step, standing face to face with our squad leader the look on his face would have caused grown-up men to mess in their pants. "You didn't have your fun for a month and so. My gift," he told me, staring straight in my eyes. I was dumbstruck, then slowly raised my left brow, smirking a bit.

"Can I have my fun?" I meant for it to be sarcastic instead it held rage, boiling fury.

"They are all yours," Zach slung his weapon over his right shoulder.

"Can I make it more fun?"

"Be my guest," he took a step to leave then retreated again, to face me. "Make it quick," was his curt reply. I nodded flashing him a grin and turned to look at the monsters, not removing the smile on my face.

Without saying a word, tossing my rifle for Troy, who caught it effortlessly, I grabbed my pistol, pulled the hammer back, and fired. Their yell filled the room. I didn't flinch as hot blood touched my combat boots. Shooting both in the leg was just a starter of what I had planned for them.

"How does the pain feel? Fun ain't it?" I growled bending down so our faces were at level. The one with dark black eyes chuckled, spitting blood.

"Not as much as what I was doing to that whore," he retorted, throwing his head toward the poor woman on the bed. I didn't move my eye contact, standing up, then raised my right hand, which held my gun, and hit him hard on the head with the rear of my pistol. A sickening sound satisfied me.

I cursed, gritting my teeth, such rage was understandable, but right this moment another face flashed before my eyes, the difference was she was soaking in rain, was younger than this woman. "I'll make sure to show you what fun is," the voice that sounded from my mouth was deep with emotions as I replaced my gun then took out my black knife; the rabbit's eyes widen making me smile in satisfaction.

"Hassan, come join me," I spoke loudly tossing the handle of the knife from one hand to other.

When we done with them, there wasn't any need to look in their faces, as a soldier I knew I could handle blood but if someone were to see it I don't think they would stay conscious for a little longer. I didn't wish to just shoot them and get it over with. Those animals deserved the worst.

For the last touch up I once again grabbed my gun and shot them straight in the head, both fell with a heavy thud on the floor, on their blood bath. The feelings that were running inside me were tough, urging to do more to them but that would be insane. My hands were bloody, so were my boots and pant. I didn't care all I knew this moment was they were dead and trust me this was the first time in my life I actually felt at ease by killing them.

"We have to move," Troy said when I wasn't moving my eyes from the dead bodies in front of me.

"What about the lady and the kids?" Hassan questioned cleaning the blood from his hands on the curtains.

"Take them with us, choppers will be here soon to take them back to the camp," said a voice behind us and now I turned to see Zach stepping in the scene. He didn't look at what we had done, stepped over the blood and stood by the bed, where Carlos was checking on the women. I had forgotten about him.

"How is she?" our squad leader asked, hiding the women with another sheet because the winter cold was brutal.

"She is coming around, once she wakes up we'll leave," Carlos replied, cleaning the blood from her face with a wet clothe.

"I'll give you five minutes, Carlos, we have to move," Zach then turned to us" Get ready," with that he left the room.

"What are you going to do about the bodies?" Hassan raised his eyebrows.

"I don't know, let them here what other option we have?" I replied walking towards the lady's closet, opening it, trying to find some warm clothes for her. Soon found them. The problem was how are we going to give this to her? At times like this I really wished we had a female soldier in our team. With a sigh I placed the clothes on the bedside table that's when the lady opened her eyes.

Turns out the little boys were her kids. Her husband had left them to fight for his country, leaving her with her older son who was ten and the little chubby boy who was only seven. Surprisingly she didn't scream and yell at us when we told her we have to leave her house her reply was 'I knew you were the good guys' this hit all of us hard in the chest.

When we left her house it was afternoon, even with the sun smiling lazily down at us it was cold, extremely cold. Every time the wind blew it felt like someone was cutting your skin with a cold knife the only difference was no blood was flowing. Finally, we decided to rest and were ordered to rest behind a broken wall of what seemed like a shop. Soon a small fire was put on giving the kids some warmth.

Having those kids around sure scared the shit out of us but everyone seemed to be at ease, even Zach the moron. He is a father and I'm sure those boys reminded him of home, his family. Noah the little seven years old was always around Troy and Hassan, while Ivan the ten years old was mostly around his mother, giving her water, and protecting her from us. He had witnessed his mother being tortured by the looks of it the young boy knew what they were doing to her, after his father he was the man of their little family. The lady was scared of us but trusted us blindly. She kept her distance yet was around us.

Noah was sitting on Troy's lap, with his dirty, torn clothes, eating Bruce's crackers. His hair was greasy, from the cold the kid's lips and hands had cuts on them. The kid was chubby unlike his older brother Ivan. He was darn cute and hyper all the time.

I smiled looking up at Troy, who had his long arms wrapped around Noah, chin resting on Noah's head. Troy was smiling, grinning actually. Noah kept munching on the crackers like there was no tomorrow while Troy played with his greasy hair. The kid then started rocking back and forth enjoying the comfort of the man.

Meanwhile Hassan and Carlos were helping Ivan with their food. Ivan was worried but his mother gave him an approving look which said we were not dangerous. Carlos then aided Ivan's wounds the kid was hurt badly. It angered me. The poor family didn't deserve this.

Soon it was dusk, who was welcomed by the purple sky, opening its doors for the night. The sun was yet to hide completely behind the veil of mountains so its eyes still shined on us. Giving refugees what they needed by that time Noah had forgotten about his earlier experience. I leaned back on the broken wall, rifle propped against the wall. Legs straight in front of me and ankles entwined.

I watched Noah tugging on Hassan's combat pants, the boy reached his knees. I heard him begging Hassan to play helicopter. Now this I really wanted to watch. Hearing his brother Ivan ran up to them, eagerly demanding the same. I chuckled. Hassan grabbed Noah's small, chubby hands, then started spinning him a feet above the ground. Chuckles were heard when Noah began to laugh. Ivan was getting impatient for his turn. So Carlos the big guy went up to him then played the same game with Ivan.

When chaos is all around us, we find peace in the simplest thing; today we were blessed to have those kids with us. It's been a week since we came here, not even once any of us smiled, this felt good, real good.

Two days since the kids and their mother left for the camp. We had been going further in the city. Last night, around 3:00 in the morning it was snowing, shocking us all. By the time we woke up in the morning to leave there was no sign of snow at all like it was a dream or an illusion. The cold had picked up its cruelty, freezing us on the place. The exposed part of my skin soon felt raw and numb as we kept walking down the road. My back was bent a little against the bitter wind.

I was aware what was going on around me but a large part of my brain was thinking about her, about Avalina. Every time I closed my eyes she was there, every dream I had was shared with her. I knew exactly what I had to do.

Chapter 17

- -

"Yes sir," I saluted. Zach nodded and walked away from us.

Troy whistled, "You requested to patrol on the camp," he teased. I raised an eye brow. "What are you going to do?" he further asked, stealing a quick glance around us. It was afternoon, nothing out of usual same old camp, but it was cloudy. We had at last returned, as soon as we were done with the formalities I requested to patrol at the camp. Zach was curious but the Bull never loses a chance to make us work.

"What do you think?" I deadpanned, wearing my cap. He laughed, giving me a look that said 'I know your secret'

"I'll catch some rest, you go do whatever you want," with a wave he went inside the tent.

Excitement bubbled in me like a volcano as I turned and walked toward Avalina's tent. It's been days I haven't seen her, my heart was lost in the desert, desperate for something to drink in, and only her face was the answer.

I passed two girls playing something I couldn't really get, smiling up at me and simultaneously saying something in their language I couldn't understand either so I waved. "Blade," called a voice, and I turned around to see a friend of mine in another team walking toward me.

"What's up Garnet?" I shook his hand.

"Some girl was looking for you, asked if I have seen you," Garnet told me.

"Who?" but the answer came in my mind and I grinned. "Where did she go?" I questioned him, hiding my eagerness.

"I saw her going back in the medical tent; she seemed rather disappointed when I told her I have no idea where you are,"

"Thanks man, I better go and check what the girl wants, hope it's nothing serious," I said then walked straight for the medical tent. We had been apart from more than four weeks. I desperately wanted to see her.

The smell of medicine welcomed me in the tent. There were patients, searching around she wasn't here, so I got out of the tent, took a turn and there they were. Fiona was talking to Avalina, with her back to me. Her head bowed as though in defeat. Slowly walking toward them, flowers all sort of blossomed in my stomach. Ignoring everything I looked at her. Oh God how much have I missed her!

Fiona grinned when her eyes fell on me from the looks of it they both were arguing about something actually Avalina was complaining about something. I put my finger on lips for Fiona to pipe down just for once she obeyed surprising me.

"I asked two of his friends, even Troy, he said Blade wasn't with them, there was sadness in Troy's eyes which meant..." I heard Avalina trail off, when I was only two feet behind her.

Fiona played along calmly, "What? So you mean..." she said, a glint of playfulness on her face. I wondered how Avalina missed it. "I am really sorry," She tried to sound a little more hurt. Avalina nodded, and I knew she was on the verge of shedding tears.

"The last time I saw him, a month ago, I really wanted to tell him something, something I wanted to say from a while now," then a sob escaped her lips. "He said he would return."

That's it, I couldn't see her cry now. I cleared my throat, and her body went rigid when she realized my voice. Slowly Avalina turned to face me, when her teary eyes met mine, the card house came falling down. I drank in her appearance, and my dreams did great injustice to her beauty. The innocence that called for me. Her eyes, those eyes that drove me insane, and left me in the midst of misery were looking at me and hell I knew she was feeling the same, because right that moment there was no one except us. The walls I build up to keep my distance fall apart. All that happened in just a second.

"Blade," she murmured like she couldn't trust her eyes, then catching me by surprise she threw her hands around me. It took me a few seconds thought before I engulfed her, wrapping my arms protectively around her. Stroking her hair which had grown nearly touching her hips, "I missed you." those three words meant more to me than anything in my life. Hell, having her in my arms felt more to me than I can ever explain.

We stayed like that that for a while, and then I felt her getting uncomfortable, maybe she had just realized what she had done, but she didn't know how that made me feel or how much it meant to me. I brought her closer to my body, inhaling her scent. She had nothing to be afraid or shy of. This time she didn't hold back, and let me hold her.

After another moment of staying like that, she finally pulled away; "I thought...Troy said you weren't here. I thought something happened to you. I thought you were still angry with me," she rambled. I smiled, "I am so happy you are fine," Avalina finished, leaning back so she could look in my eyes.

Fiona smiled and walked away giving us some privacy. I'll thank her for that. I looked down, still smiling. "How are you?" I asked her. Avalina wiped the tear that fall on her cheek.

"Better now," I had a feeling she had lost all composure, she was saying words which if she would say a month ago she'd either blush or feel uneasy. I smiled at her, she cleared her throat, "When did you come back?" And asked pushing her hair behind her ear.

"Just about an hour ago," I replied, taking her small fingers in mine, and tugging her gently away from there.

"Where are we going?" her voice filled with curiosity, but she still tightened her grip on my hand and followed.

"Somewhere quite," I led her around the tents.

This was my secret place, nothing special just grass hidden in some trees and bushes not many people came there. We sat on the soft grass, still not letting go of her hand. It felt right in my hands. We sat in silence, listening to the birds singing. The wind dancing around us. I wished, Dear God I wished to hear the words I have been craving to hear, every moment, back in the war.

"You must be tired?" She began looking at our hands entwined with each other. I stared at her.

I was, I really was but I didn't confess it 'cause seeing her had taken all the fatigue away, "No, not really." I lied, "It's good to have a little peace at times like this when I am with you." I murmured, looking at Avalina as wind teased her hair, taking a note of how her soft cheeks colored at my comment.

"So...Err...How was the war?" She asked, nearly making me laugh. I raised an eyebrow, at that question.

"The war...umm... It was bloody, sweaty, despite the freezing cold, brutal and extremely exhausting." I didn't realize I had been frowning. "All in all, it was my full fun package with only one thing missing, your presence."

"Is that your way of saying, you missed me," She joked.

Then I smirked, "You think?" she flushed red again making me laugh.

"So, what is it?" I asked after a while. She looked up, frowning, clearly confused. "I heard you had some confessions to make."

"What confessions?" I knew she knew exactly what I was talking about but she was acting dumb, trying to run from declaration, but she didn't know I wasn't going to give up so easily.

"I just over heard you with Fiona. You were supposed to tell me something a month ago." I hinted trying to make her feel at ease. She didn't reply, and then I carried on with a drawl. "So?"

She was taking deep breaths, exhaling them. I just watched her, not smirking I knew she was nervous as hell and confessing was a big thing for her. If I teased her she might not tell me and that I swear to whatever is holly will kill me.

Avalina bit her lip again. "I... don't know where to begin with," she trailed off dropping her gaze. I gave her hand a gentle squeeze. It was surprising the hands that held, guns, bodies; RPJ'S can be so gentle when it came to her.

"I wasn't sure of my feelings, but now that I have learned what I feel, I am scared." her words were in a rush but I heard them loud and clear. My soul was at last at peace. "The thing that held me back was my own self. When you showed me your care, I thought it was you sympathizing with me, but then you confessed." She paused for a minute. "I was shocked at first, thinking how someone like you, a soldier, could be interested in me? I had nothing else to give you in return, unlike the women you might have known back home." I frowned at those words; she had no idea what she was saying. I haven't been seriously involved with anyone from years.

"At first when you told me how you feel and then you left I had planned to tell you that I am no good to you Blade, you deserve far better than me. I have nothing to give you." She gave an exaggerated sigh; "What could I possibly give you in return." She sniffed, as tears rushed in her eyes. I could take anything the world throws at me, but those salty tears in her eyes were unbearable to bear for only two seconds. I waited for her to speak; she looked like she was holding on something big. And she was going to break down any moment.

"I have had people that I loved and have lost them too, I hope you understand." I nodded for her to carry on. I have spent half my life without a mother, I think I know how she feels. "I couldn't allow myself to let you in, I had closed all doors but you managed to sneak in." She shook her head and shrugged her shoulders. "But then I grew selfish, I realized I couldn't help it. After a week of your departure I began to miss you, unconditionally." Now she looked at me as though she was in a mental fight with herself.

"Ava..."I started; she gently raised her right hand. "Let me...I'm not finished yet," I nodded.

"All this time missing you made me realize yet something else, something I thought it was impossible for me to feel, losing my family had shattered every part of my heart but then you were there, you brought them back, a rush of feelings, they were escalating in my heart, my brain would disagree with my heart and then eventually they started to walk on the same path, with both my heart and brain on one side how could I be on another! " she finished, looking in my eyes as more tears escaped her eyes.

I leaned in cupping her beautiful face in my hands and placed a kiss on her forehead, then on her eyes.

"Ava, I wish I could take you away from here, and spend the rest of my life with you but that has to wait just for a little while. Back in the midst of war every time I pulled the trigger it was with more rage and pain. There was more desperation and need for revenge. Then one night," I snaked my other arm around her waist, "I asked my heart 'Why it is my feelings are foreign to me?' It replied the answer is simple in every bullet you see her face. I asked my heart again. 'How is that possible, how come I am unaware of my heart?' It didn't reply just simply remain silent. Once again I questioned my heart. 'If I am unaware of my feelings you are my heart, you know everything' it smiled replying, 'I am not yours anymore, Blade"

"I was silent for a minute. Then it spoke, 'I belong to her, I've belonged to her the very moment her green orbs meet your blue ones, Blade, but it took you a while to understand' it left me speechless. Then the truth came rushing down to me that I am addicted to you. Addicted like the stars to the sky, like the beautiful moon to the glorious Sun. Like the trees to the peaceful wind, like a stupid heart, to its beats, Ava I am addicted to you," my voice was small, lips against her eyelids. I touched her chin with my left hand, while the right one still around her. I heard her sigh in relief and pulled away smiling. Shoved my hand in my pocked, then pulled 'it' out of my pocket. I closed my fingers around it's chain and held it in front of her.

"What's that?" She demanded, curious with a beautiful frown on her face. I opened my palm, where sat a pendent, a heart in a heart attached together. They shined as the sun pushed the cloud away choosing the perfect moment to glorify the beauty of the pendent even further. I looked up at Avalina.

"It's beautiful," she praised, glancing at me then at the pendent. I told her to turn around, she blushed causing pride stir in me. I gathered her hair gently; they were soft just how I like it, pushing her hair on her right shoulder, I hung the chain around her neck. On purpose brushing my thumb on her skin. I almost growled when she turned to face me again, her fingers touching the hearts.

"Thank you," Ava spoke and before I could reply she leaned in dropping a kiss on my cheek. Holly shit! I froze. Yeah, I did. If anyone were to touch my heart it was beating itself like a drum. She was grinning down on the pendent, the wind making her hair dance once again. That moment I knew I was darn lucky to have her by my side.

She looked up at me again, "Where did you get it from?" I smiled sheepishly. She raised a delicate brow.

"Well we were patrolling so there was this jewelry shop, it was destroyed, everything stolen, no one was there. My eyes fall upon this, hanging from one of the shelves so I grabbed it for you," I smiled.

"You stole it!" She gasped, touching the hearts again. I smirked at her and leaned back on my hands.

"No, I didn't steal it. I just borrowed it," was my reply. Avalina narrowed her eyes. I found myself looking in them.

"Blade I am being serious here!" Avalina scolded, I couldn't take it anymore so I laughed while she glared at me.

"I am telling the truth Ava, if there was anyone I would have paid them some money, besides I deserve a white gold pendent for what I am doing for their country," I told her, grabbing her hands, drawing circles on her skin with my fingers. Ava exhaled then nodded.

We talked for a long time after that. She smiled and listened to what I had to tell her about death angel (my father) she seemed to have respect for him, saying he is my father must be some amazing person. I agreed but wasn't going to say that. She wanted to know about Maya, I told her everything she needed to which made her feel like they could be great friends. Never get why women say they will be friends when they haven't met!

I even told her that I'd told Maya about her when I had the chance to talk to my sister weeks ago. Ava blushed murmuring something I didn't catch. When it came to her Ava talked less I knew she didn't want to talk about her family yet she tried to tell me.

Too soon it was my time to patrol here in the camp, no matter how much I want to be with her duty is duty. Besides that idiot will literally kill me if I don't show up there in five minutes. I sighed, reluctantly letting go of her hands. Avalina looked up; reading my expression a sad look crossed her eyes when I stood up.

"Come here," I gently demanded. She stood up, looking up at me. I couldn't help but to smile down at her. Removing the hair that touched her cheeks I let my lips brush against her forehead. "I will see you later, please take care," were my parting words to her. She nodded giving a small smile then walking where I had brought her from.

Chapter 18

"Don't let him go," Troy barked at the others, who were holding me in a firm grip. I struggled but it was all in vein, because they were holding my legs and arms, trying to put me on the ground. Other soldiers were gathering around, making a circle to see the show.

"Let go man, I swear when am free am gonna kick you all in the arse," I shouted but there was laughter in there.

"Pipe down," Hassan the second mastermind behind this was holding my hands said, with a grin so wide it was almost a miracle his lips didn't tear.

"This is our treat for your promotion, Blade," said Carlos, keeping his weight on me as they put my body on the ground, others let go and backed away only a step or two. When I tried to push Carlos back and stand up, at once something white was poured on my face. Now Carlos stood up and barks of laughter sang in the air. Seconds later, something cold hit my body, followed by dirt. I squirmed, hiding my face with my hands, which spread the shaving cream all over my face, covering my light stubble and lashes.

"Congratulations' man," Troy chuckled joined by laughter of others. I lay there laughing as they emptied the cans of their shaving cream on me. I guess they'll have to borrow other team's shaving creams tomorrow.

"Now the best part," Carlos chimed, grabbing my shoulders, standing me up.

"Oh no, you don't," I yelled, struggling, but Carlos got a hold of my hands behind my back.

"C'mon ladies, we have got ourselves a punching bag," he gave the green signal for the other almost twenty soldiers around me. I glared as Hassan stepped up, first shaking my hand congratulating me, then I huffed as his fist made contact with my chest.

"That hurt," I huffed, making him hit his knee while laughing.

Again, laughter rang around me, but I stood still enduring the punches on my chest. This was some sort of a promotion ceremony, no not the main ceremony, in which the higher rank would put a medal on our combat shirt. Whereas the boys had something unique in mind, like showering me with shaving cream, dirt, and water then to make it even better-delivering punches on me. Bloody cowboys!

Troy stared at me no expression on his face. His eyes spoke everything. He was confused, angry, annoyed and somewhat proud. "You did it man," he at last spoke, breaking the thick tension between us. I gave a nod.

"They were considering it during my duty here on the camp," I explained feeling a little anxious.

"They did the right thing," he delivered.

"You ain't mad?" I raised my eyebrows.

"Nah man, I knew your promotion wasn't far away. We all know you sort of worship this job and work hard for it." he cracked a smile. The annoyed expressions all flew away. I was confused then it hit me.

"Oh c'mon man! You were faking the drama all this time," I growled making him laugh. When we came back at the camp, Troy was sort of off, I thought he might be pissed off turned out I was wrong.

"Blade, you're a moron to think I'll be mad at your promotion, dude am your bro," Troy said then gave me a hug patting my back a few times.

"I am happy, am sure your old man is flying right now,"

"I am sure he already knows I was promoted," I told him when we parted.

He nodded," This is good, now you're a rank higher than mine," I laughed saying, "Soon you'll kick Zach, and be the Sergeant,"

"Yeah, but he'll be something else," Troy grimaced and then chuckled. "Wish we could celebrate,"

"Now, I don't think so. Besides you were more than happy to shove me around in the promotion ceremony," this made him laugh as the memories of an hour ago rushed in.

"It ain't funny, you grabbed my hands behind my back, and all you idiots punched my chest. And you," I pointed my finger at him in accusation.

"Delivered a punch harder than anyone," I glared but knew there was a smile in my eyes.

"We had worse plans for you," he snickered.

"What's worse than you ruining my suit with crap while I was on the ground?" I demanded, turning around and sitting on the plastic chair.

"Well...we wanted to wrap your body with duck tab and leave it out in the rain," I knew he was trying hard not to laugh.

"Oh I'm glad you didn't cause once I was out of those duck taps I would have kicked everyone who was in this prank with you," I threaten, then ended up laughing. "It was fun, I am glad everyone had something else to think about,"

"Zach was proud of you," Troy said sitting across from me.

"I'm sure he doesn't want Colonel to see how wants to punch me in the face,"

"Maybe," I knew Troy wasn't jealous but it made me sad he wasn't with me. Everything that happened in life it happened with both of us. At least such big occasions did. Things were changing little by little and I didn't like them.

It was raining fast, the drops hit my face softly, as I stood there in the cold night, outside the medical tent, brushing off the insane wind around me, which stuck my clothes to my body almost making me freeze on the spot, and still I waited patiently for Ava to come out.

We were here for four days, every day my every spare minute that I had, I spent with Avalina, even though that meant having a little sleep, but I didn't care. I just wanted to be with her, wanted to know her more, being around her felt so, so right that leaving her was agony. Tomorrow my team was moving out again. I couldn't wait to spend more time with her.

I was in my combat suit, without the helmet or rifle, desperately waiting for her to come out now. Troy was resting back at the tent; apparently, he also wished to patrol here keeping me company. So, I waited welcoming the cold rain. I shifted my weight to my other leg, and that's when the flap of the tent opened as Avalina rushed out and then walked toward her tent.

Shading her eyes with her right hand, she jogged. I followed, somehow feeling like a stalker, but I was far from it. Mud splashed on my shoes, we passed tents and I was almost behind her. There was no one around us, which was something I was glad to have. I noticed her wearing the shirt I had given her months ago; the fabric was clinging to her body, water dripping. I feared she might catch a cold. Well I was soaking wet and I didn't give a shit about it, all I wanted right now was to be with her.

Avalina turned another corner and I followed soundlessly. Then I quickened my pace was just a feet or two away from her. I grabbed her wrist and spun her around. Avalina gasped, was about to yell, but when her eyes fell on me, she threw a hand over her mouth preventing the scream from cutting the air.

"Goodness Blade, you scared me," she scolded, freeing her wrist and taking few steps. I sighed and once again spun her around to face me, this time snaking my left hand around her waist, bringing her closer to me. Ava gasped, eyes growing wider.

I studied her face, the wet hair that stuck on her beautiful face, the green eyes looking at me, worried, shy and confused. I raised my free hand, whipping her hair away from her face, loving how she blinked four times in just two seconds. The whoosh of the wild wind around us was forgotten for that moment, the thunder that stuck, illuminating the dark sky was ignored, and the merciful rain that drenched the world had no value to us that very moment.

"Ava," I begin in a slow voice, it was deep with emotions, which were no longer foreign to me.

"Ava, I am leaving tomorrow. I wanted to be with you, wanted to spend my time with you," I told her, staring down in those eyes. Avalina bit her lip, dropping her gaze.

"When will you come back?" her voice was barely a whisper, just like mine. I pressed a kiss on her forehead, holding her tighter in my arms.

"I don't know Ava, a month or two. I can't tell, but I have something to ask of you, something I have been thinking about from a while now," I informed stroking her cheek.

"What?" she murmured, her voice muffled in my chest. I pulled her away, and looked deeply in those eyes that dropped a brick in my stomach, swell my heart and teased my dreams.

"Ava tell me how much do you care for me?" How much do you want me in your life?" I demanded gently. She laughed; it was like a ringing wind chime.

I saw her narrow her eyes as she organized her thoughts and then she spoke with sincerity; "How much I care! I could have died, but your team saved me from the cruel fate, when the other man tried to help me, I saw 'them' in his eyes though he was a good man. Nevertheless, when you tried to calm me, your eyes they begged for something, the purity was poured down into rivulet from your eyes. I agreed, then once again," she cleared her throat, trying not to frown.

"You and Troy saved me from that vicious man, I felt great amount of gratitude toward you, I was horrified," she smiled again, shaking her head as though at a memory.

"You were like a cloud shadowing me from every danger that lurked there. You stood like a mountain in front of me all the time. My heart was already yours. There are no words in the world that can explain how insanely I care for you. You ask how much I want you." She raised both her eyes brows a glint in her eyes, a glint that said she meant every word, making my heart run fast; thunder stuck that moment giving me a clear view of her face.

"If I spend another day without you I can't live. I don't know how I will live without you, Blade. I will surly die," she finished desperately with her bottom lip quivering, she bit on it. Her words hit me like a storm, only God knows what they brought in my heart.

The tears in her eyes were not hard to figure out even with the rain pouring down on both of us. I bent down and kissed her eyes, then the tears on her cheeks. She had told me before how much she cared about me and I am sure she knows how much I loved her.

Wild bushes danced around us, there was no on around at this hour. Only us and the nature, which gazed at us with awe, Avalina wrapped her hands around me, feeling her fingers tighten made feelings rush in me, she was driving me insane with her simplest touch.

"Ava...In the time of hell you have showed me heaven. When there was no one you became my life, my everything, in the time of war you gave me peace and I would always want that, my love for you never dry's, in fact it grows more in my heart every day, every minute and every second. Until it consumes my body and soul, then I will kneel and will give myself away to you." I tipped her chin up, caressing her cheekbone; she shivered.

"Ava, will you be with me? Avalina, will you marry me?" I asked slowly, staring down in her eyes, aware of the lump in my throat. The fast running of my ticker and feet going cold. Deep down inside I knew the answer; still I was worried, waiting for her reply.

"Blade," she sobbed, pressing her head against my chest. My pride swelled making me grin. Right now, I was the happiest man on the face of earth. I had God to thank for this. She pulled away; looking at me with so many emotions in her eyes it was amazing. Amazing the girl who hid her emotions could express them so loudly without uttering a word. A bridge was crossed and pages were turned but we kept staring at each other as if nothing existed in the world around us.

She smiled a darn cute one. "So is that a yes?" I raised my eyebrow. She shook her head.

I smirked, "A no?"

She shook her head again. "A million times yes," and laughed, I joined her. It felt good to be around her, like all the problems in the world vanished being near her, like I was melting in her embrace in her eyes just like butter on a hot toast.

My hand left her chin and encased her hand in mine,

"Come with me," I said tugging on her hand.

"Where?" She protested lightly.

"To show you heaven," was my reply, which made her blush.

Chapter 19

- -

The clouds were pouring down on us, hard and fast, like their heavy sheets were mourning for the ones who had lost their lives. The trees danced in the wind of sorrow, rustling its leaves as it did. A huge light struck high in the sky yet it felt so near, making the clouds cry even harder. The flowing water had turned into crimson as it flowed from the shoulder of the road and carried its own dark story. I blinked my eyes and looked away from the red water.

Troy was yelling at me, saying something constantly, but I couldn't hear at all, nor could I hear the roaring of guns all around me. The blasting bombs, the screams of people who breathed their last. I simply stared at Troy, with his rifle in his hands, blood dripping down his cheek, soaking his shirt along with the rain. He had dirt on his face and a terrified glint I could see burned in his eyes. His lips moved but no sound came out. What was I doing? Am I dreaming? If the scene in front of me was of war then why am I not moving? Why am I not feeling anything? Why am I not doing anything?

"Blade..Blade," a distant yell reached my eyes, making me frown. Troy glared at me then pointed his finger on something, desperately as though time was ticking. "Blade, wake up," Troy hollered again, and then it hit me like a hurricane.

Everything was real! This shit was real. The dreadful voices made me flinch. I tightened my hand on something, which turned out to be my rifle. Here I was, with my back pressed against a wall, rain pouring down on me and with Troy still yelling at me. I turned my head to where he was pointing at and death crawled up my heart. Almost fifty of them were engaging towards us, they had two tanks along with terrorists in cars, our cars! I dragged my eyes from them and looked around me to see that there were only six of us against all of them.

"Blade, take your position," Troy called for me. I blinked, making the raindrops fall on my face. From the corner of my eyes I noticed, yet once again, the small river of rainwater mingled with thick, dark blood around me. A ghost of windswept the street sending leaves swirling high above the street. I blinked yet again, kicking in every battle instinct in my body, straightening my spine. After grabbing a magazine and reloading my rifle, I embraced myself for the worst.

Everyone here knew we had no chance in surviving that. Zach had already been calling for backup, standing in the ruins of a library, with rain showering and fifty men charging toward us- towards six soldiers. How did this happen?

"Troy, I need you to stay here back up Blade and Bruce. Find a place to hide and engage. We have to hold them for as long as we can. I am leaving three men here and three soldiers on that building, attacking from two places will confuse them. You three cover our backs and each other, hurry!" Zach yelled over the angry voices.

"The backup team will be here soon, 'till then give your best," Zach barked his last words then darted toward the destroyed building next to the library.

"Blade, C'mon man you have to gather yourself," Troy encouraged standing next to me, pressed against the wall. We were on the first floor of the library; the reason why we were on the first floor was because there were no remains of the second. This place was burnt to ashes; the sky could be seen clearly from where we stood. The windows in front of me, from which I had seen the enemy, had its glasses shattered by a bullet.

I frowned at Troy's words, 'Get yourself together, but why?'

Bruce, the third man in our team, sat behind a pile of bricks and ruins which I remember we had created as a trench for him, taking hold of the machine gun we had placed there earlier. At once memories flashed back, before hiding here, hiding in this destroyed library. We were attacked by another group of terrorists, throwing grenades at us. I had been caught up with them; with my body paralyzed the team had killed them all and dragged me here, and stood me up against the wall!

And here we were in combat with death itself. I looked at Bruce, who started praying. Thunder struck, I looked up and smile appeared on my lips as Avalina's face appeared before my eyes, her smile, and the soft voice she spoke in, her hair that teased my face whenever she was in my arms. That was when I felt my heart being torn from my chest, squeezed until the pain was unbearable.

I looked down, noticing the rain drops that dripped from my helmet. "Use every bullet you have wisely, every time you pull the trigger aim at someone, kill them, embrace your strength, and embrace your death for this moment. We are here to serve our country, our people, and our loved ones! Its do or die," I yelled every word, loud and clear, with sincerity, with respect and with courage. I had no idea what would happen.

Looking at Troy, I grinned, giving his shoulder a pat. "Let's have a bet, let's see who will kill the most," I represented, he smirked, but sadness was visible in his face.

"You are on, man," he winked, walking to stand in front of me, with his back against the wall, so that we were facing each other.

"Get ready," Bruce bellowed. My heart skipped a beat, and started trashing against my chest. With a deep inhale, I drew my rifle, looking death in the eyes, tightening my grip on it as they came nearer. The good part of this, the killing, the bullets crying all around you, the people dying, the stream of blood, was that their numbers have decreased a great extent, which means there is hope. We could win.

I glanced at the building Zach was hiding in, waiting for his command. We could try and hide and let them pass, but that would be an extremely stupid move. However, with them surrounding us it would be hard to engage. The way they were charging toward us, we could easily get killed. We have figured out, a long time ago, that they are skilled. There are high chances they have predicted we had a hideout here.

For that we had to wait and see.

When only forty feet away, Zach ordered, and that's when hell broke loose. I pulled the trigger, aiming at the ones who were walking. They swiftly stopped their vehicles, taking position. Just like I told my team members, every bullet was to be aimed at someone, to kill. The enemy hid behind their cars which now had our unmerciful bullets pierced in them, creating a bee nest. As soon as those monsters took shelter behind their cars they drew their guns on us.

Our negative points were the tanks they had as sidekicks. If they were to target at us, we are done for! The enemy quickly figured out our hiding points and started firing at us. We killed almost fifteen of them but it was far from ending. This shit just got started. The constant blazing of guns had my heart beating so fast that it was a miracle I was still standing. Everywhere I glanced; it was mud, blood, and water. This place was the ultimate mark of chaos.

An ear-piercing blast sounded and one of their tanks ignited into flames so large that it engulfed the building nearby, making the people flee from there, giving us a chance to target them. As soon as the flames started we knew Zach's team was the one that had fired a grenade.

The sky cried even louder making it hard to see. We were facing the power of nature as we fought while sheets of rain fell from the sky, as if the tension in the air had wrung the moisture out of it.

"Loading," yelled Troy to me so that I would give him back up. A bullet wheezed so fast and hit the wall near me. I could almost see it ripping through drops of water. I glanced toward the source.

They were advancing, clearly coming from around the ruined buildings on the sides. "Shit, this is bad," I turned my gun toward the five men only few feet away from the library which had no walls from sides, or a roof. Pulling the trigger, I didn't miss at the start but when my foot slipped because of the mud beneath my feet I did miss the other three.

"Bruce keep shooting from the front, Troy back him up. I'll take care from the sides," I shouted, not removing my eyes from the enemy. Everything screamed of disaster, death lurked in the corners as the enemy kept advancing.

Suddenly the earth shook with such mighty force that it took a second for me to recover. The other tank had shot a shell for the library, which tore the air with amazing speed.

"DOWN!" screamed Bruce, letting go of his machine gun to duck in the trench we had made. Troy and I threw ourselves on the ground, resulting in mud splashing all over us. The shell hit half of the library, shattering it onto dust, revealing us to the naked eyes.

We lay low as dust rained on us. Troy and I then stood up, visible to everyone out there. A small hill of bricks was on my right so I ran for it, throwing myself, and pressing my back against the broken pile of brick. Troy joined Bruce in the small hole and began firing again.

A stinging pain on my right calf made me realize it was wounded. Ignoring the oozing blood, I turned on my stomach and crawled a few feet top of this small hill. Wincing at the wailing of the guns, I placed my rifle on top of it, then pulled the trigger again.

One down,

Two down.

The numbers increased, but it was never ending. There was no other feeling in my heart except for the extreme horror of dying. My heart was running against time, every fiber in my being was begging for this to just end. But not before I make them kiss dirt; not before I kill them all.

I felt my face pale, despite the cold weather which had numbed it, when I heard our team leader, Zach, screaming in the radio.

"Soldier down, I repeat soldier down!"

"God!," I roared, avoiding my shaking hands. Bullet after bullet passed me every second but I didn't retreat. "Loading," I yell out for backup while reloading my rifle. My head snapped up as a bullet hit the rock in front of me. Swallowing the lump in my throat I then found out it was dry, with a mixture of dirt and blood.

Chapter 20

- -

I won't lie by saying that my legs were not weak from fear. When death sucks the oxygen from your lungs the best of the men, have their walls of strength crumbling down.

Now we were five against many of them, chances of living were down to zero. Two of the enemies were coming towards Bruce and Troy, firing like maniacs. I turned my rifle toward them, pulling the trigger, the hot bullet whizzed through the air, and as the fog hit it, it turned to steam. Their yells reached me as the bullets cut deep in their flesh and blood splashed from the wounds. Ignoring them I turned the tip of my rifle again toward the crowd in front, and then my whole body jerked from the force.

It was like someone had shoved a burning rod in my shoulder, pain hugged my left hand and the shoulder burned. The red blood that flew like a snake from the wound had splashed on my face and lips as well. Gritting my teeth I blinked many times because of the hot water swimming in my eyes, not from the fear but from the unbearable pain. My breathing was shallow and I could feel sweat trickling down my back, despite the rain. I licked my lips, pushing the fire that ignited in my body aside.

"Loading," Troy's yell shook me out of the trance; I brought my rifle near and crossed it against my chest, holding it near, as my left hand was unbelievably weak. I have been shot before but this was different, maybe because I knew death was mere inches away from me!

The bullets that shot from my rifle shook my wounded shoulder, making me hiss in pain. The water and sweat that dripped from my head burned my eyes; I had to flatter them violently to clear my vision.

"Bruce is down! "I heard Troy yell in a desperate voice, my head snapped in their direction in time to see Bruce fall backward in the trench with a bullet in his head, and his helmet rolling away. I cursed my luck and this situation. Quickly grabbing my radio I yelled in it, "Soldier down, Sarge, we have a number down!"

"Blade, hold them back a little longer, the freaking backup is almost here," Zack screamed back. I didn't reply back because that very damned second, I dodged intense fireworks which were directed at me. Ducking behind the pile of bricks, my chest rose and fell rapidly and adrenaline pumped in my veins. Constant whizzing from bullets and pinging from ejected clips had almost come into a rhythm. Screaming and yelling echoed and as if to add to the battle sound the sky cried louder.

I opened fire on them and heard Troy yell. "Blade, get over here now!" he threw a quick glance at me.

"If I move I'll be dead," was my reply as I shot another in the leg, when he fell on the ground my bullet struck him in the chest! A huge blast sounded, I turned around to see the tank was on flames.

"Hell yeah, that's right," and yelled in triumph, crouching down as hot bullet casings rained down on me.

Looking up at the sky, clouds were still crying, with intense force. Ever since I was younger I always believed rain was lucky for me. It soothed the anger and pain in me, and would put out the fire in my heart. The sound of the thunder made me smile when I could barely walk, it still does. I prayed continuously that this rain would be lucky for me, that I would be able to see Ava, my little sister, Maya, and my old man.

The enemy was dangerously close; we were almost running out of luck. "I am out of damn bullets," Troy barked, tossing his rifle aside and taking hold of the machine gun.

"Where is the backup team?" I shrieked grabbing a grenade, pulling the lock then threw it toward them. A moment later I heard the blast and then started firing again. My gaze fell upon a group of people advancing fast for us. My heart wanted to tear my skin and jump out of my chest. Troy wasn't paying attention to them as he kept shooting in front.

I couldn't move if I did I would be dead the moment I turned my body, and if I sit here like a pathetic coward, Troy my brother, my comrade would die. I can't let that happen. A few horrific seconds ticked in which I debated.

"Hell with it," I hissed then went for it. I had to. There is no way on the face of the earth I won't try and stop death coming for him when I knew where it was coming from. My heart was trashing against its cage as I stood on my shaking feet, then darted to where Troy was, ignoring the flying bullets and the guns pointing at me.

I reached, throwing my body in the trench, and quickly turned my back on Troy. "I've got your back, let's get them," I shouted over the maniac chaos, aiming my rifle at the group coming from the west. A thunder struck that moment showing the puny humans its power. Once again a skull-ripping pain traveled through my shoulder and I almost gave away on my rifle. This was hard, very hard every second was like a day, and every attempt was fatal.

I sucked in a breath through my nose and tightened my grip on the rifle with shaking hands. My kidney cried in pain and energy was draining from me with every passing minute. In a split second, I glanced down to see blood spreading on my shirt. Dear Lord! Gritting my teeth I tried as much as I could and carried on with what I was doing. Once the last man of the group that was advancing from the west was down, another group of monsters appeared. "This is not happening," I quickly threw my empty magazine and reloaded. "Troy, we got company," I yelled, over my shoulder. Standing with my back pressed against his.

My knees were shaking uncontrollably, but with tremendous effort, I managed to keep on standing on my feet. I had to. Troy needed me. I braced myself and drew my rifle with my dirty and wounded hands, my breathing fast.

"We can't hold them back," Troy screamed.

"We don't have time to argue like a wimp Troy, just kill," with those words I shot a terrorist.

Time stopped as two helicopters hovered over us, and snipers targeted those animals on the ground. The backup team was here! We were safe; there was a big chance for us to get out of here. Relief spread over me and I thanked God for sending help. A smile spread on my lips as I shot down another one.

But then....as though I had woken up from a dream, he looked at me, straight in my eyes, anger, rage burning in the iris of his eyes.

He pulled the trigger. I blinked, simply blinked, as his body fell in the pool of his own blood. Everything became death silent, it was over, and we'd killed them all......

I coughed and spitted blood, and with a sway my body fell in the trench. Troy turned to look at me, frowning, his gaze dropped down. "Shit!" he yelled, dropping on his knees next to me.

"No, no, no," he cried his eyes wide, quickly grabbing my numb body and pulling me out of the trench, then lying me on the mud. Troy undid my bulletproof vest and tossed it aside. His eyes narrowed at the three bullets that pierced deep in my body and the warm blood flowing from them.

"Blade you are going to be alright," he promised. I tried to speak but again coughed blood. "Shit," I heard him curse, grabbing my shaking hand, then giving it a squeeze, the pain that spread in my body was indescribable. My lungs were on fire, suffocating me, and every breath I took hitched; it was like my body was being torn on nails as they dragged me, ripping my skin and organs.

I felt helpless as I tried to grab the fading light when the darkness spread around me. I gasped for gulps of air. Hearing my friend yell when I turned to look at him, a tear caused by the pain rolled down my eyes, and I blinked. My lips queried when I looked up at the sky, blinking once again when raindrops fell in them. I shut my eyes tight, struggling with all my might to prevent a shriek of my own from escaping my lips.

"It's cold," I whispered, my voice a squeak.

"Blade, come on man don't give up," Troy hissed desperately. I could note the shake and fear in his voice. Looking up at the gray clouds a weak smile made its way on my lips. The rain beat down on my face as I smiled, for the first time in a long time, as a free man.

Then I saw her; saw Avalina's face appear in the clouds. I wanted to reach and touch her, but my hand was too heavy to move, she smiled back at me with a glint in her enchanting eyes, I tried yet again to raise my hand and touch her, feel her soft skin but failed. Panic chocked my neck as her face started to vanish and I couldn't take it, I had to see her, she couldn't leave me.

Flashback.

I buried my face in the nape of her neck; the skin was soft, so soft that it felt like silk against mine. The faint scent of roses engulfed me. Her back was pressed against my chest, while my hands wrapped her in an embrace. We were sitting in our place, the place which was blessed to me, where she had confessed her feelings for me. Ava had said she cared for me, that she trusted me!

I smiled against her skin, she laughed. "Your beard is tickling me, Blade," I chuckled and nuzzled my cheek against her skin once again. She squealed pulling her neck away. I smirked then raised my head, placing my chin gently on top of her head. Ava twined her fingers with mine and played with them.

"God knows how much I wanted this moment with you, Ava," I murmured watching the sunshine peak through the trees and smiling as the leaves swirled in the winter wind, and the humming of it wrapped her hair around my neck.

"You did?" she asked, drawing circles on my hand.

"Every day since I met you, every night when I dreamed about you. I told you before you drive me insane, yet keep me sane at the same moment," I explained, bringing her closer to my body. Her warmth was intoxicating. It felt warmer every time I hugged her.

"Seems like I am an interesting person," she teased, then laughed. I was silent because I wanted to hear her laugh, wanted for time to stop.

"You are," I said in a whisper and placed a kiss on her hair. Time ticked and we sat like that, in each other's embrace and loving the cold winter. Something came in my brain and I smiled again, a memory.

Last time when I told Avalina I was going away for another week or two it had been hard and exciting. I had never seen her act like that; it was as though a new Ava was standing in front of me. I remember perfectly.

"You are going again?" she had asked, not sad, not disappointed but angry.

"I can't help it, they need me," I took a step closer to her. Ava held her hand up.

"Blade you just came today, you can't go back! I haven't seen you for days! "Her voice rose and a deep frown appeared on her face.

"They want me and I can't sit here and ignore my duty. You know that," I told her gently. She shot me a glare that left me baffled, Ava started pacing in the tent, and no one was around us so it was safe, it wouldn't matter anymore everyone knew about us. I watched as she paced, running her hands over her silky hair. I sifted my weight to my left leg and watched in utter amazement as she turned, tossing her hair aside which had cascaded on her shoulder in the act.

Her mouth opened and she talked and talked and talked. I seriously had no freaking idea what she was saying. Avalina started pacing again, throwing her hands in the air now and then, glaring at me then huffing.

"Why are you looking at me like I have grown two heads?" She demanded and now I blinked.

"I didn't get a thing you said, Ava" I chuckled.

She frowned "What do you mean?"

"You were lecturing me in your language, Empana language" I smirked. She bit on her tongue.

"I was?" I nodded, and stepped toward her; she put her hands on her hips and lifted her chin. I crooked a finger at her and ushered her" Come here."

"No," Ava said, turning to leave. I shook my head and grabbed her waist. "It's not fair," she protested. I sighed.

"Ava, don't make it hard for me, please," she stared at me for a long time, then gave in.

"Just this once," I chuckled and wrapped my arms around her but like I always say fate plans something different, Aden had walked in on us and ruined my moment with my girl. I glared at the boy but he ignored me totally, little prick.....

"Blade, Blade," her voice brought me back I looked down and her eyes clashed with mine. "What?" I asked, and she sighed.

"I have been calling you for a while you were so lost,"

"Oh sorry Ava, I was thinking about the time you lectured me in Empana language," she blushed.

"Don't make fun of it, I speak in my language when am upset or angry,"

"I know Ava, I know," I smirked, bringing her closer again, feeling her soft body against mine. "So what were you saying?"

"I was saying tell me about yourself, about your life back 'home"? When those words were said, pride rose in me. She had considered my home, hers.

"Home,"

She gave a hard nod "Yes home,"

"As you know my father, he is 'The Marshal' of our army and my sister lives with him, sometimes I stay there with them when we get back from a mission, but I have a house of my own, given to me by the army, It's always empty." I stopped and thought about what I was going to say next, knowing well that she was waiting for it. " I would like someone to wait there for me, someone to smile up at me when I enter the house, someone to spread happiness, and love in the house, someone that could shield me from my own despair,"

Ava turned her head looking up at me, with feelings so intense burning in her eyes that left me befuddled."Will you share it with me?" Her voice shook with the feelings that burned in her. I could read it in those enchanting eyes, could see it clearly on her face.

Leaning closer, I placed a kiss on her cheekbone. "You already share my heart, Ava, you're the only thread that keeps me alive and I want to live there with you," she shivered from my voice and wrapped her hands around my neck.

What happened between me and her after that is a secret. A secret I will never forget.

End of Flashback.

"Blade, look at me, they are here, you are going to be alright," Troy's voice brought me back, cupping my face, turning it on the side so that I could look at him.

"It's too late," I gasped, with all the strength I could muster. I raised my left hand, resting it on my stomach and felt warm blood around my fingers. My eyes watered again as another extreme wave of pain hit me. It was like the bullet was traveling in my organs cutting them down in pieces.

"I don't have much time....."I stopped and pushed my ring with my thumb from my ring finger. Troy grabbed my left hand once I had started taking off the ring.

"Blade," he growled. I swallowed, tasting my own blood, and then turned to look at my friend, my brother. Troy had tears in his eyes. I wanted to smile; it was almost funny he had never shed a tear in his life.

"I.I can't take care of her anymore; I don't trust others with her. Troy, I never asked anything, please, promise...me," I coughed gritting my teeth as burning rods were shoved in my neck.

"Don't say that. Don't you say that," he hollered. I slightly shook my head and placed the ring in his palm, his hurt face killed me. I was sorry for everything. Sorry for things that turned out to be this way. Sorry for leaving him alone and facing the world. Sorry for myself. Sorry for Avalina. What was she doing right now? Probably helping the patients, my sister, Maya, dear Lord I was sorry for leaving her alone. I wanted to see her, wanted to see the shadow of mother in her face.

Everything was getting dark and I wanted to escape from it. "Troy, promise me," I begged, ignoring my burning throat. He looked angry, torn apart. "I don't have much time," I choked.

"You shouldn't have come there, you should have let me feed those bullets, Blade you selfish moron," Troy grumbled, bowing his head in defeat.

"I knew I was going to die Troy. Just..."I trailed off unable to complete.

He nodded.

"Anything for you my man, anything," he promised as his voice cracked, with my shaking hand I gave his hand another squeeze and looked up again at the sky. Avalina's face appeared, she smiled down at me, my bleeding lips twitched a bit, my body was cold, very cold and everything was getting quieter. I felt Troy tighten his grip on my hand as my eyes closed and I welcomed death.

'I guess this rain wasn't as lucky as I thought........'

Chapter 21

He grabbed her hand and gently dragged her, "Where are we going Blade? Avalina asked, trying to keep up with his long strides. Her feet hit hard in the mud, which in return kissed her shoes, making her grimace in disgust.

Blade turned to look at the woman who drove him insane, "To show you heaven," His comment made her blush, and Avalina duck her head, making her wet hair stick gently on her cheeks. Blade looked over his shoulder once again, while walking. He wanted to reach and wipe those strands away from her cheeks, though he loved her hair, they were silky and soft but it annoyed him when they disturbed his view. He wanted to see every inch of her face. She was his drug, his addiction.

When Avalina raised her head, she frowned at the sight that welcomed her. Where was he taking her? To the tent and at this time! 'What about all the soldiers resting there?' She thought to herself urgently and opened her mouth to question Blade. Before she could utter a word, Blade gently tugged on her hand, pushed the flap of the tent and walked in. Avalina's eye widened, when she saw almost seven soldiers there, few of them were resting while others were talking in hushed voices, they all looked up at them at their approach, and Avalina hid behind Blade's massive body.

"Where's Fiona?" Blade questioned, walking forward, not letting go of her hand. He knew she was terrified and utterly confused as to what was going on.

Hassan stood up. "She will be here," then he looked passed them and smirked, "Think of the devil and the devil is here," Fiona rolled her eyes and ignored Hassan's taunt, smiled brightly at Avalina who was watching everything with big eyes, amazed, and a little bit scared.

"So, she said yes?" Fiona inquired, coming to grab Ava's hand.

Blade nodded proud and happy, looking down at Avalina, aware everyone was looking at him, but he didn't care, he knew the power his heart had was stronger than his doubts and fears for their relationship, and tonight he had proved it, proved how much he wanted her in his life. He smiled and looked at Fiona "So where is Troy?" he asked, looking around.

"Ah! I was wondering when you'll be free from staring at Avalina and look for me," Troy rose from the cot he was resting on and smirked at his friend. "Glad to know you still pay attention to your surroundings, Troy," Blade chuckled.

"Blade," a small voice called for his attention. He looked down at her and frowned, because she was terrified, her eyes shown with question and hesitation "What is going on?" Avalina's small voice pushed the frown from his face; he stared hard at her, at her beautiful face. She was scared he could see it in her gaze.

"You agreed to marry me, right,"

She gave a fierce nod, making her dripping hair bit on her eyes "Yes I did Blade, but what is this?" Ava asked again, sweeping her eyes around them in an urgent manner.

He stepped closer and bent lower, so that she won't raise her head higher in order to meet his gaze "We are getting married, right here, right now," Blade came clean, waiting for her reaction. He watched as her green eyes widened, and she gasped.

Blade cursed himself for being so stupid and naive. He had just thought about himself while dragging her here. He wanted to marry her and make her his. Looking at her, at the tears that rushed in her eyes, and biting her lip in utter confusion. He begin worrying, what if she didn't agree to marry now? What will he do? What would he say to all the people around them?

Avalina looked around them, and realization hit her hard. The men around were Blade's team members, and Fiona was here to help her. They were here to be the witnesses of her marriage to Blade, but was she ready? She saw Troy looking at her, with a small, gentle smile playing on his lips then her eyes landed on the man who stood there, waiting for her answer. Was she ready?

Blade has always been there for her, every time she needed him, he was there, powerful and tough. Like a mountain, he stood in front of her, shadowing her from the danger Lee had showered at her, from the people who had killed all her family. It was he and his team members who protected her. She stared at him, her heart did a flip, shocking her, it started beating fast, her gaze flattered a bit, and thoughts ran in her brain. When her brain showed her the image of how he had asked her to marry him. A blush burned her cheeks so she dropped her eyes.

The fast beating of her innocent heart only proved her doubts. She started shivering, though she wasn't sure if it were her wet clothes, the dripping water or the way he kept staring at her. Avalina looked up. She knew she was ready, with him she can have another life, with him she will be happy, live a life she lost, months ago. She gulped, and nodded.

Blade smiled, when she gave a nod of her head. He grabbed her soft and small hands in his, and faced the crowd waiting for them. "We are ready," he spoke proudly.

"Took you long," Hassan chuckled and added, "So who's going to be the priest?"

Carlos stepped forward, seeing as his father was priest, he knew how it's done.

"Perfect," Fiona clapped her hands. "Blade and Avalina come and stand here please," Fiona requested, as she stood next to Carlos. Doing as they were told, Blade still didn't let go of her hand and walked to stand in front of Carlos, his team members standing on both sides.

"Wait, Blade you are forgetting something," Troy spoke.

Blade turned right to look his friend in the eyes "What?"

"The rings, what will you do about the rings?" Troy reminded resting his hand on Blade's right shoulder. Blade frowned, trying to think of something.

"Tie a small piece of clothe around your fingers," Hassan suggested. Everyone shot him a glare; except Avalina, who blushed scarlet. She didn't know who they were and it was her first time being around them and she was getting married, but every time she glanced at them, the men who were tall, broad and dirty, smiled at her, like a daughter, like a sister. Their eyes spoke of their feelings and Ava felt welcomed. She felt save.

"We have to have rings," Carlos spoke, growing agitated, his jaw tightening. Silence passed and everyone racked their brains. The rain hit hard on the tent, making Troy frown as they distributed his concentration.

"I don't know how you men work in a squad without a woman," Fiona sighed with a shake of her hand, then as everyone watched she took off the ring she was wearing in her index finger and handed it to Blade. He looked up at her, then at the ring, unable to say a word. The ring was simple, very simple with just a small blue rock as a decoration in the middle.

"Fiona, I can't take this, this was your sister's," Blade started to argue. Fiona glared at him, and then moved her gaze to Avalina and her eyes softened at once.

"She is my sister too Blade, she is getting married and I am not going to let some ring ruin this beautiful moment at a time of war. Come on now," The doctor dismissed, not removing her eyes from Avalina.

Blade looked at Troy who shudggered, he wanted to punch him in the face, right this moment he wanted Troy's suggestion and he just shrugged. Blade couldn't take the ring, he had to come up with something else, but what?

"Quit thinking so much Blade," Zach the team leader and Sergeant spoke for the first time and every attention was on him, even Blade was shocked. The man was only here because he wanted to see if Avalina was marrying him for any greed, right now Blade knew Zach had gotten his answer. What shocked everyone was when he removed that plane silver ring from his finger and placed it next to Fiona's ring. "I always wear that ring, it brings luck, don't worry it's not my wedding ring I keep that in my bag," Zach said with a light smirk on Blade's expressions.

"Sarge..."Blade was unable to compelte because Hassan butt in with his great remarks."Damn and I thought I was emotional," this made Zach chuckle, he looked at Avalina. Who knew this was the man who made Blade suffer the most.

"I am handing a man from my squad to you, I hope you make him suffer more than I ever did," He joked making Avalina smile a little. Zach stepped closer and patted her head like a father, which almost brought more tears in her eyes. "We are ready, Carlos," Zach ordered.

"Yes Sarge, I mean Zach," he smirked then began with the ceremony.

Blade grabbed her hand giving it a light squeeze letting her know he was there for her, that he will always be there for her. She had his beating heart and everyone knew, they were witnessing it right now. She was going to be his wife and his forever. The thought of her being his, brought so much pride in his heart he thought he might not handle it.

He looked at her while Carlos talked, she was shy and he knew it. He could not keep his eyes from his Bride. She was so beautiful it destroyed his sanity. Blade kept staring while Avalina payed attention to what Carlos was saying, like it was the worlds most important thing, but for him it was she, the way a single drop of water dripped from her hair and trickled down her cheek. His eyes followed lost in thoughts, in her beauty. Every glance he took at her, Blade took another vow to protect her, to cherish her every day.

And then came the time for the vows, Avalina couldn't say any-thing, she just watched Blade. Her heart was filled with so many feelings they were confusing her. Ever since Blade entered in her life, things stabilized. She had lost everything, her family, her faith in life. That day when she had been brought to this camp, Avalina had tried to find a way to kill herself, lingering around in the night, looking for something. She did not care about the rain that had been pouring on her, or how badly her injuries hurt, all she wanted that moment was to find something to finish her life with.

Before she could do anything, or register the situation in her mind. Lee had appeared in front of her. Avalina still remembered how terrified she was, she knew at once that Lee was drunk, and tried to flee, but her injuries has planned something else. That was the reason why Lee had wrapped his filthy hands around her, making her scream in protest. She wanted to die in peace, in dignity this was something she had not thought about.

And then there he was, just like the first time. How she looked at him, in his eyes and pleaded for help. Avalina was hurting all over, and her brain was tired, tired of the things that were happening to her. She tried to push Lee away from her, but the man was like a rock even in a drunken state. She couldn't take it. All she saw was his angry eyes, eyes that promised protection, with that she had given in.

Her heart did a flip when she remembered the time when he gave her his only shirt. That was her turning point that was the day she thought may be God was giving her another chance to live. She knew Blade had feelings and they were pure toward her. The only problem was she couldn't return them, her heart had turned into coal, but when standing on the hill, seeing him smile at her turned the pitch black heart into a beating one, like waking up from centuries of sleep.

Her throat went dry when Blade said his vows, every eye was on her. Her heart was beating like a drum. Avalina dreamt about her wedding day, wearing a white gown and facing the man she would love with all her heart. She had dreamt about saying her vows in her language. All that were childish matters for her right now. The white dress, the man of her dreams, the language. It was Blade that mattered and her vows to him, and she was ready to say them out loud.

A tear rolled down her eyes, as she started saying her vows. She missed her mama, her papa, her sister. She needed them here. More tears rushed in, and Blade wrapped his hands protectively around her as though reading what was going in her mind. She finished her vows and watched with wide eyes, as Blade gently pushed the ring in her ring finger. A sob broke on her lips.

"Avalina if you are going to cry we will think you don't like him," Bruce told her gently. Avalina gave a short nod and bit on her lip. She took the ring from Troy's hand with hers shaking, not out of fear but out of love. She never thought she would be loved so much that there would be no place in her heart.

She tried her best to stop the tears, but failed. They were tears of happiness and she had no control over them, slowly she grabbed his hand and pushed the ring in his ring finger. Avalina looked up at him and passed a small smile. The crowd broke in congratulating him as Carlos announced them as husband and wife. Hassan wolf whistled and gave Blade a hard pat on the back. When it came Avalina's time, he simply smiled and caressed her hair, like a sister. Fiona pushed him aside and wrapped Avalina in her arms.

"He is yours now, all this time I have been trying to get him away from danger, now I give his responsibility to you, Ava," Fiona whispered in her hair. Ava nodded and looked at Troy who waited for his turn.

Troy cleared his throat, because it was his first time after Blade had threatened him to stay away from her. He was feeling a bit awkward. "Never thought Blade would find you here, I am glad he did. Don't worry if he makes you cry I'll make sure Blade pays for it, now you are not just his wife Avalina, you are a member of my family," Troy smiled, grabbed her right hand and placed a soft kiss on her skin.

The team members congratulated both of them, Blade wrapped his hands around her waist and brought her closer, he was happy; his heart was at last at peace. He gave Zach a nod without saying a word, both man had an understanding. Zach had played a role of father for Avalina and Blade was glad to have his team captain here with him.

"I have to tell Maya about this, I am sure she will go insane," Blade whispered in her ear. They were still in the tent; he had wrapped her in some blankets and made her drink some tea.

Avalina looked up and laughed silently. "I hope she does not get angry at you,"

Blade shook his head, " She won't I have already mentioned you many times, I am worried she might fly and come here," he chuckled, pushing a strand of her hair behind her ear, the hair were getting dry and he worried she might catch a cold.

Blade didn't know what future had planned for him, he was happy he was with her; he had everything, her smile, her heart. That was what he needed; ignorant of what life had planned.

Chapter 22

I stood there by the door of the church watching the pallbear-ers carry the casket out of the church and waiting for her to walk out with Maya, but Avalina sat there, not caring about anyone. She was silent all the time; we hadn't heard her say a word since we came back from Empana two days ago.

The country was free after our troops had killed the terrorists in a great number. They had surrendered to Empana's government and next day few of our troops were sent back home. Marshal, Devin had demanded his son's body to be deported to him as soon as possible. I was one of the few who had left Empana the next day and had demanded for Avalina to come along with me, as everyone knew she was Blade's wife.

One by one people left, Maya glanced at me and I shrugged having no idea how to deal with Avalina, the girl upon hearing the news of Blade's death hadn't even shed a single drop of tear, all she did was remain silent and lost in her own world. It was terrifying to see her like this and the thought of something happening to her scared the hell out of me. I had just lost my brother, my friend and losing someone as dear as Blade will destroy me. Swallowing the lump in my dry throat I made my way toward her.

Avalina was staring down at her ring, the ring Blade had shared with her and made her his wife. Thinking about him made something tighten in my heart, making my already dry throat go drier. I stood next to her, but she didn't look up as though there was no one around her. People had been looking at her with questioning eyes, and I knew Devin would demand for some explanation as to why she is here, but he did not know it was his son who has given his life to this girl.

I bent down in front of her, it was a wonder how she couldn't hear my heartbeats, worried, confused and lonely. "We have to go," nothing, she didn't even raise her head, so I tried again. "They will bury the body, you have to be there," nothing just the silence that the church carried. I wanted to grab her shoulders and shake her out of that world, but dear Lord she was fragile and on the verge of breaking down, doing this would only increase her pain.

Then she stood up, clenching her hand and I knew she was going to break down any second, her lower lip began to tremble as she started walking towards the door of the church. I followed silently close enough to catch her when she needs me. I wanted to curse, yell with all the rage burning inside me. He died in my hands, in front of my eyes leaving me with his love, leaving me with another duty to protect her! If only I could protect myself from what is to come in the future.

I watched as she slowly descended the church stairs, the wind blew around her, hard and fast bringing news of rain and storm as more clouds engulfed the sky. There was no one around us, people were getting in their cars, and pallbearers were closing the door of the vehicle in which the body was placed.

Suddenly Avalina stopped, stared at the car as the engine came to life and doors closed, her eyes grew wider and a sob broke on her lips.

"No!" I heard her beg, with that things happened too fast. I didn't have a chance to register them. She began to descend the last stairs fast and run toward the car.

"Shit," I cursed and ran after her; it was as though all feelings had returned, as though Avalina was a human again. I quickened my pace as she kept yelling after the car. My shoes hit the grass and I ran after her. Once only a feet away, I grabbed her shoulder gently and twisted her around to face me.

"Avalina stop they are gone," I shook her shoulders. When her eyes met mine I felt my insides going rigid. I knew it was then she realized Blade was gone, Blade was dead!

"Let me go! Please I beg of you let me go," she struggled.

"You can't do anything Avalina," I tightened my grip a bit. Tears rushed down her eyes like a stream and that very second the sky broke loose and began crying, mourning Blade's death. She trashed violently for me to release her, but I couldn't. The wind blew her hair and echoed her desperate yells.

"No, no he can't. Tell him, tell him to wake up and stop this act," I frowned at her words and then they hit me like a storm and I had to drop my gaze, it was unbearable to look in her eyes when she was looking at you as though you are her only hope. Help me dear Lord.

"Tell him it's enough, he can wake up. Troy I beg you please tell Blade to stop acting. I learned my lesson, tell him this is enough he can come back, he has to come back." she sobbed harder grabbing my hands. I turned my head from Avalina because I couldn't say anything it was as though my tongue had rolled back.

"I can't Avalina, he is gone, and Blade won't be back." I told her gently and swear to God it took all my courage to say it, ignoring the flip in my stomach.

Tears streamed down her eyes when I said those words she shook her head violently "Stop lying! He is not! Blade said he will come back. Stop those man, stop them, they can't just take Blade away from me. "Avalina spat in a harsh voice and began to pull away.

"Let me go!" She screamed, desperate and I pulled my hands back like they were on fire. She didn't run simply started walking down the grass, she was letting the reality sink, I could see her body shaking from shock and apprehension, when her legs weren't able to carry her own weight she came falling down to her knees. I ran to where she sat on her hands, staring ahead at the deserted road.

Her sobs died down and she kept staring, staring at nothing specific. Avalina had lost the man who cherished her in a place where death knocked on door every second. She lost her husband when it hasn't been two months of their marriage. I knew her eyes were picturing the three bullets that had pierced Blade's body, the blood that had painted his skin. I followed her and went to sit beside her.

"He is gone," I grabbed her hands. "You have to know this, Blade. Is. Dead," I almost yelled those words. She flinched retreating her hands and buried her face in them. The clouds kept crying, mourning his loss with us.

I ran my hand over my face and wrapped her terrified form in my hands "No don't. He is alive, he promised," she struggled but I tightened my grip around her.

"I am sorry I couldn't save him, I am sorry I didn't bring him back, Ava he loved you, he loved you so much," with those words she turned her head and buried her face in the crock of my neck and shed more tears.

If this is what happens when you loose a loved one, I pray I don't have one!

They were honoring Blade's body; the casket was placed in front of us in the graveyard. Avalina sat next to me, she did not say a word to anyone, and only God knew what she was going through, even if I tried to imagine her pain it was impossible. Blade was her world; he was her light, her strength. But who said if the body has died his memories will too?

I didn't leave her side at all, no matter how many duties I had. Zach made sure my work was given to someone else so that I would devote my time to this girl. No one questioned about Avalina's presence, Maya wasn't in the state to ask nor was Devin. As the Marshal of army he made sure to show no emotion at all. It was almost shocking seeing Devin have a straight face.

Soon the ceremony was over. I grabbed her hand and we stood up, people were laying roses on the casket and I knew Avalina didn't have the power to bear it, so I gently tugged on her hand and walked away from them. We were walking when someone interrupted us. It was Blade's aunt, Jessica.

"Mrs. Parker," I begin as she stood in front of us. "It's been a long time."

"It has," she murmured then said what she had stored in her heart. "Oh! Troy I am so sorry, my son," She wiped her fallen tears.

"He won't be forgotten," I said. She nodded and her eyes fell upon Avalina she frowned.

"Who is this young lady? I saw her with you earlier as well," Mrs. Parker interrogated, before I could reply or utter a word she answered shocking us all.

"His widow, I am Blade's wife," Avalina choked the words as fresh tears burned her eyes. Mrs. Parker's eyes widen in shock.

"Dear Lord! My dear child," she wrapped her hands around Avalina, who didn't react at all. I didn't let go of her hand either. "It will be okay. God is merciful; He will take care of you,"

The tears that were threating, escaped her eyes as they parted. "Come on let's go," I reminded, squeezing her hand, the hand which was once held by Blade, and walked to the car.

When we reached Devin's house, people were everywhere. We walked inside and I turned to face Avalina. "Sit here. I have some people to meet," I told her in a small voice, she gave a nod and sat on a chair. I just hoped she won't cry again, because there were pictures of Blade everywhere in this house.

I met all the soldiers who had come to honor Blade. 'Marshal' was glad I was next to him. Maya was trying to accompany the ladies, I recognized her as their mother's friends. They were close to Maya like Aunts. She needed them today.

Hours passed I still couldn't find a chance to go back and check on Avalina, people were finally leaving slowly and finally I was left alone. I quickly walked where I had left her, glancing at the clock, it was six thirty at night, she was no where in the living room, and there were only two guests. I looked at the backyard, found Maya but Avalina wasn't there either. Anger rose like a volcano inside me.

What would Blade think that I already lost her? Blade....Of course. Darting inside I took two stairs at a time, turned right stopped at the last door in the hallway.

The door of Blade's room was ajar, there was a small light, illuminating the room and I knew it was the bedside table. Swallowing the lump in my throat I stepped in and found her, sitting on the floor, near the bed, holding the picture I had taken when Blade had graduated from college. She was crying silent sobs shook her tiny form. I sighed, walked to where she was and sat in front of her. "Avalina," I spoke softly.

"He asked me to marry him the last time he was there." her deep voice spoke, breaking the silence. "I agreed, I agreed because I thought I would live a long life with Blade, but I lost him, he was there only a day with me, I lost him," she wept, hugging the frame closer to her body.

"Avalina," I called her name and walked the last steps towards her. The tapping of my shoes rang on the wooden floor. "Please don't cry." I knew those words irritated her now. "I know him and I am sure Blade would hurt seeing your tears, would hate seeing you cry," I consoled wrapping a hand carefully around her shoulder.

"Why did this happen to me? I lost everything and now I won't see him ever again," she traced her fingers on the picture.

"God loves you, He is testing you! He has things planned Avalina so please don't cry," I pleaded. She sniffed as her bottom lip shook and more tears rushed from her eyes. She cried for a long, long time, in that time the poor soul had leaned on my arm for support.

Memories of how he met her flashed before my eyes, how Blade had protected her from Lee in the camp. How he always looked after her, even on the battle field he was lost in her thoughts. Now seeing the love of his life break into pieces right before my eyes, it took a great amount of will power to not break down.

Her breathing became slow and deep. I looked down to find her eyes closed, she was fast asleep. I exhaled, trying to take the frame but her grip was firm around it. I gently wrapped her small form in my hands, slowly picked her up and rested her on Blade's bed, then covered her body with the covers.

"God help me," I murmured looking at her, feeling like something inside me was perishing.

I waited a minute or so there in-case she would wake up or need something but then remembered Avalina was tired and needed all the rest she can get so I went downstairs to talk to Devin. He was sitting in his study, with his head in his hands; shoulders sagged in defeat and sorrow.

"Sir," I called in a whisper. Devin looked up at once all the emotions hiding away.

"What can I do for you soldier?" his voice was stiff, I frowned.

"Nothing Sir, I was here to talk an important matter with you," now it was his turn to frown, looking straight at me, and his gaze penetrating just like Blade used to say.

"It's about her," he said through gritted teeth.

"Yes sir. I have wanted to talk to you about her," I told him, still standing.

"Well have a seat then," he gestured for the chair in front of him. There was a moments silence between us and I tried to calculate every move.

"How did Blade meet this girl?" he asked not removing his eyes from me.

"Avalina, sir was one of the hostages we saved, our team," then I told him everything he had to know, every detail. How he married her the last days on the camp. Devin remained silent, raising another wave of anxiety inside me.

"You were there when he married her?" I nodded.

"I was one of the witnesses sir, our whole team was there,"

"How can you be so sure, may be this girl wanted my son to get her away from her chaotic country," he snapped. I narrowed my eyes.

"Sir the war is over in their country."

"Many soldiers have been used that way," he spoke, clenching his jaw.

"Blade was the one who started this relation sir. Avalina had seen her family being slaughtered right before her eyes, Blade was the one who took interest in her," I told him with great caution.

"How can you be so certain?" he demanded, frustrated.

"Sir, you are well aware of Blade's friendship with me," I argued, not in a bit ready to give up, not when someone's life depended on me so I kept going on. "You can investigate Private Carlos and our team leader, Sergeant Zach," he looked at the table with a deep frown.

"It is hard to believe," Marshal murmured, hands clasped.

"It's true," spoke a voice from behind me. I turned to look over my shoulder. Devin looked up to see Maya, standing there. We knew she had overheard our conversation.

"What do you mean, Maya?" Devin interrogated, sitting straight.

"I mean everything Troy said, is true," Maya answered walking to sit next to her father.

"What makes you say that?" Devin asked again. He adored his daughter and would believe everything but I was a bit confused here as well.

"Dad, it had only been three months when, he, Blade called me. He told me everything about Avalina, asking for my permission. I was happy to hear that and agreed, agreed for him to take another step, by that I meant for her to be with him," Maya stopped as tears stung in her eyes. Devin stared at his daughter and his control snapped, shocking me. Seeing so many emotions cross his face. I felt sympathy for him and understood why he hid those feelings. Being the Marshal of army those feelings weekend your status.

"It is true then?" He asked his daughter once again.

"Yes dad, it is," Maya sobbed, wrapping her hands around herself. I had hard time breathing.

Devin stared in the space for a while and my throat went dry. This was exactly how my man Blade would think, staring in the space to concentrate and consider all the possibilities in front of him, coming up with the best solution.

"I would like to meet her; it seems my son did choose her for his bride. If so she will be under my protection and will live with us," Devin declared, his voice had turned soft. It was my first time hearing him call Blade 'son'

"As soon as she wakes up, sir," I replied. He nodded and stood up, vanishing from our sights.

Chapter 23

Avalina

It has been three devastating and lonely months since Blade left me alone. I was living in his house, the house he told me we would live together in; that he would like for me to welcome him with open hands but now here I am completely alone! He was everywhere, everywhere I glanced, and Blade was there. I felt abandoned at times that I wanted to grab my heart until it stopped beating. He haunted my dreams, even though I didn't know how he died but I kept dreaming about his death. I knew Troy was with him and that was what I dreamed about. Every time my own yells would wake me up from my nightmares, they were the reason I couldn't sleep. Seeing his face like that was horrifying. I was scared of him, yet I wished so much to see him again.

Losing him was like every part of my body was aching, like someone had tore my chest apart, grabbing my heart to cut it in half, placing it back in the wound and bleeding so much that my soul was drenched in my own bloodshed.

His family, Devin and Maya cared a lot for me but what was I able to give them in return? Nothing! My life was upside down. I did nothing but to shed tears. Maya said to take the pictures down from the walls but I felt like she was taking my broken soul away. I couldn't say anything but cried, seeing me, vulnerable and shattered Maya took pity. I know she wanted to help me with everything; we sort of became sisters just like Blade had once predicted.

Thinking about him was like suffocating yourself, then again there wasn't any day or minute I wasn't thinking about him, killing myself again and again. It was like you were drowning and only his memories would save you. I remember him saying something to me like it was yesterday. "My love for you will never die; in fact it grows more in my heart every day, every minute and every second. Until it consumes my body and soul, then I will kneel and give myself away to you." Those were the words he'd said while asking me to marry him, and now I understand what he meant by love growing with passing seconds.

Silent tears escaped my eyes as I wrapped my hands around myself and his smiling face flashed before my eyes. I would give anything, anything to touch his face again, to feel the warmth of his embrace.

"You're crying again," said a familiar voice. I turned around to see Maya there with her hands crossed with an eyebrow raised.

"I am sorry," I replied, quickly wiping my tears.

She sighed and came forward, "I don't want you to cry anymore, you have lost all your weight and its scaring me," she wrapped a hand around my shoulder.

"It's hard," I murmured, ducking my head walking down the hallway.

"I am sure my brother wanted you to be happy, please don't hurt him more, your feelings are destroying your health, you're not eating not taking the pills," she argued gently, following me.

Even though Maya was just a year older she was just so motherly it was welcoming. At the start I was reserved and didn't open up to her, but with time it was impossible to ignore her.

"I will try Maya I will, but it's really hard there is like a hole inside my brain and heart, no matter how many years will pass the hole will be exactly the same," we had now stopped in the living room.

"Ava dear, you can't always live like this," she told me firmly.

"I don't want to move on, it's impossible," I turned my gaze away from her intense one. It penetrated the walls of my strength.

"It's not impossible, I know how much you love him-" I spoke before she could complete.

"I do love him, I did love him and will always love Blade for the rest of my life," now my voice held a harsh edge.

"I understand it but as his sister I can't see you like this," Maya literally growled, she had indicated many times for me to move on but today she had enough of my mourning.

"I want to live like this, here with him" my voice quivered.

"Avalina you are not with him, he is not here! There might be someone waiting for you, someone who can make you happy again," she kept going on. A sob broke on my lips and I shook my head in disagreement.

I couldn't take it; the thought of being with someone was utter torture. "I can't," a tear fell on my cheek as I looked down. My heart was beating extremely fast. The sheer thought of someone being near me scared me; I felt my hands getting sweaty, lips going cold.

"Why can't you? You are still young," she spat, growing frustrated.

"Maya I can't, stop please," I begged, taking a step away from her, as though she was hurting me.

"Avalina, you know I am right! Why? Why can't you live when you are still beautiful and there is someone ready to take you? Blade is not here! Why is it hard for you to be happy again?" she demanded in a high pitch.

I felt something break in me, something I had been hiding. I heard the shatter from the distance.

"How can I?" I screamed staring in her eyes. "How can I be with someone else when I am expecting his child?" I was shaking by the time those words left my mouth.

"Avalina, you... what?" Maya gasped, looking at me like she was scared. My world went black for few seconds and I collapsed on my fragile knees, hiding my face in my hands. After a moment I felt her sitting next to me, there was no sound except from the ticking of the clock and my muffled sobs.

"Is it... Is it true?" Maya questioned in a whisper. I wasn't looking at her but knew she had turned pale. I gave a nod, hearing her gasp, then an arm wrapped around my shoulder. "When did you find out?" she was crying as well.

I swallowed looking up at her. "A month ago, I went to the doc-tor and she said it has been two months already. I was terrified I couldn't tell anyone," I told her.

"Oh Avalina! I am so, so sorry. I will be there for you on every step, my dad he will be happy to hear this," she passed a small smile. I gulped.

"He won't trust me," I bit hard on my lips. She frowned, then shook her head as though winning an argument in her brain.

"Sweetie he can make sure by doing whatever tests he wants but I believe you, I am really happy to know this," she hugged me again. I couldn't stop my tears but my sobs died down, at last Maya grabbed my hands and we stood up. She was crying as well.

"Thank you," I said gasping for some air.

"No Ava, thank you for everything," she beamed, taking my hand and leading me towards the couches.

I didn't know what future had planned for me, I only know this after Blade I have something to live for. He left me with so many memories, which were enough for a life time. I will always cherish the time I was with him, he was my life and will always be my life.

Epilogue

"**A**re you crying again?" his small voice asked me. I turned my head to see him sitting on the kitchen counter, looking at me with weary eyes. Eyes that looked exactly like mine.

"No, I am not," I lied, putting the dishes on the counter, and wrapping my hands protectively around his small body. Quickly he embraced me with his small hands and squeezed my neck. "Did you eat well?" I asked, walking away from the counter.

"Yeah, but you always say you are fine when I see tears in your eyes " he complained in my ear.

"That is because I had something in my eyes," I lied, again.

"Just like every time?" To this I wasn't able to say a thing so I didn't reply only tightened my grip around him.

"Why don't you go play outside so that I could finish my work and join you?" He laughed, forgetting everything; his innocent laugh was from heaven.

"Will you play with me?" he pulled back, staring at me with big green eyes. I nodded, making him jump from excitement in my arms, which made me smile.

I bent and put him down, without wasting another second he ran for the back yard. I sighed then grabbed the tea towel to dry the dishes.

They say when someone is gone, far, far away from your reach the memories fade away and only some linger behind, like a nightmare or a sweet dream. But I disagree, losing Blade was like I was dying every day, I missed him so much that it shattered my heart into uncountable pieces and it will take years to collect the piece back with my bleeding hands.

It has been four years I lost everything I had, my life, my soul, my love even my smile. His memories were so bright that sometimes I felt he was around me. Before meeting my husband I lost my family, losing him threw me in the world of misery.

The only reason that pushed me to live and keep going on was my child. When he was born I had something to live for. He looked amazingly like his father but not his eyes they were just like mine, not the beautiful blue ocean ones like his father. Blade's father 'Marshal' accepted me when he was satisfied. Troy made sure to stand there for me when I needed him on every step. They were so helping and welcoming.

I kept rinsing the dishes, lost in my train of thoughts that is when I heard a voice call me. Turning around my eyes fell upon someone that made me smile. Troy was here, along with Maya. I hugged him and Maya the people who were my family now.

"How are you?" Troy investigated, eyeing me. Apparently he knew and understood me more than Maya, and he always knew when I was crying even though my eyes never showed it when I shed a tear or two.

"Perfectly fine," I smiled; well at least physically my mental state was a mess. "How long are you going to stay here?" I asked as we walked out of the kitchen to sit in the living room.

"Couple of weeks," he replied.

"I came here because we have to go and shop, you know for the wedding, you are my bridesmaid," Maya smiled at me. She fell in love with a soldier, they knew each other since childhood he had asked her to marry him, and Maya agreed and suggested that I would be her bridesmaid. She protects me a lot, Maya loved Blade so much and that love was now shown for me.

"Where is our little hero?" Troy asked, looking around and I saw the new spark in his eyes.

"Playing in the backyard with the new toys his grandfather brought yesterday," I replied, looking at Maya who smiled. Affection was hard for Devin to show but his grandson brought the best in him.

Troy stood up,"Blade," when he called him I closed my eyes. I named our son after his father it brought peace to my heart every time someone called him. "Come here buddy," upon hearing his uncle's voice Blade came rushing in, as fast as his little feet could take him, seeing Blade brought smiles to our faces. God he looked so much like Blade, so much that it shocks me every time I see my son.

Blade rushed passed the tables hands stretched, Troy bent a little and picked him up. "Troy you are back," his words weren't clear enough but I understood him.

"Yeah I am, so how is our little hero?" Troy sat down on the couch and sat Blade next to him.

"Just like you had left me, I kept my promise too," Blade said enthusiastically, looking up at Troy in adorable eyes. I crooked an eyebrow. Troy glanced at me then back at him.

"You sure did," he then beamed at Blade, who started rocking his feet back and forth as he sat on the edge of the couch.

"It's ironic how attached he is with you Troy, even though you are not present half of the year," Maya stated looking up from the magazine she was reading.

"That is how it is, when you are away they miss and need you, but when you are next to them it's a different case," Troy laughed.

"Hey Troy, did you bring me what I asked last time?" Blade demanded, grabbing hold of Troy's sleeve.

"Your grandfather brought you new toys yesterday," I protested. They both ignored me.

"Yeah big guy, in fact it's in my car, go check it out," before more words were spoken by Troy, Blade jumped and darted outside. I narrowed my eyes at Troy.

"You are spoiling him," he chuckled.

"No Blade is just like his father, he gets what he wants," his smile flattered from the look that crossed my face, anxious he glanced at Maya who shrugged. "You know he would like you to move on Avalina," becoming serious at once and that scared me.

"None of that nonsense any more, please!" I said averting my gaze.

"It has been four years, how long do you plan on living your life like this?" he asked sitting straight.

"Stop it Troy, this is not the right time," Maya argued.

"No Maya it's time she should know, it is the right time, it's been years and I have to leave again if I don't tell her now I have to wait with his burden on my heart for few more months," Troy growled, at once getting frustrated confusing me. What is the matter with him?

"Troy you agreed you will tell her later at night," Maya spat.

"I can't wait," he said through gritted teeth then turned to face me, "You need to know something Ava," he called me by my nick, I frowned.

Slowly as though he was having an inner battle, he reached his jacket pocket and pulled out something in his palm.

Maya grunted in annoyance, "Now is not the right time,"

"You say that every time I come here,"

"Because I know she is not ready," Maya threw her hands in the air.

"Four years! Four years I can't hide it anymore," Troy spoke sadly.

"Yes but-" Troy shook his head for her to stop and I kept staring at them. He then met my gaze his eyes they were sad, hurt and lost.

"You need to know something," he repeated opening his palm. I gasped and sprung to my feet.

"How is it with you? It wasn't there on his finger, I thought it was lost," my voice shook as memories of his funeral came rushing back.

Troy looked at me like he was miserable, "Blade gave this to me when he died," as the words left his mouth the air around me vanished and my head felt dizzy, pushing it aside I turned to run away from them. Before I could take a step, Troy stood up in such remarkable speed, and his large hand grabbed my shoulders, gently.

"Let go you back stabbing bastard," I screamed pushing his hands away from me. He stared at me like I burned him.

"Avalina, what on earth are you saying?" Maya asked standing, she was shocked and angry.

"Blade gave him the ring, his wedding ring! Maya what is the meaning of this? How dare he say that," I hollered, glaring at Troy who simply stared back.

"Before setting your mind why don't you listen to what Troy has to say," Maya ordered, with such an intense gaze it terrified me.

"No leave, both of you. Please!" at this Troy took a step forward and looked down at me.

"I will not leave Blade's house before I tell you what he said to me when he died, and you will listen," he told me in a deep voice that reminded me of all he has done, and how pathetic I sounded at this moment cursing him for back stabbing me when if it weren't for him, I would have be destroyed by now.

Running a hand over my hair I walked to sit on my place a second or two they followed. Troy was on my right side, he grabbed my hand and placed the ring on my palm when the metal touched my skin the threatening tears escaped from my eyes and I bit hard on my lip.

"He gave that to me when he knew he had no chance of surviving and," Troy told me everything, how Blade himself had taken out this ring from his finger and handed it to Troy. Blade had made him take an oath of protecting me not just as a guardian but as my life partner. Troy even told me how Blade was worried about others, how he didn't trust other men around me. Troy was his option for me.

Sobs racked my body when Troy told me everything. I could see a huge burden was lifted from his shoulders but a hurricane was rooming in my heart. "Ava dear calm down," Maya said rubbing my hands.

"I am sorry, I am sorry I yelled at you, all this time you were keeping your word and I cursed you," Troy shook his head, stood up and kneeled in front of me, grabbing my hands now.

"No I get it, it's okay Ava trust me I feel much better seeing you angry for the first time," he said.

There was a moment's silence in which I debated on what to tell him now. He was trust worthy I knew this; my son was attached to him more than anyone, but me! I closed my eyes and pictured Blade's face, it was there so clear his memories were so fresh it would be impossible to remove them.

"I can't Troy, not now I need time please," I told him, without meeting his eyes.

Troy tipped my chin and made me look at him, he smiled, "Take all the time you need, I promise I will always be here for you."

9 781944 260415